Parent Trap

In the center of the group a caldron bubbled over a fire, and that was where the smoke came from. And to one side of the caldron four children hung aloft, tied to spears that had their pointed ends stuck in the sand. Three of the four trussed-up children seemed to be peacefully sleeping, but the fourth and smallest was awake. Now she looked down at Roger and Ann.

Ann clutched Roger. "Where have we seen that little girl before?"

"I don't know," said Roger. "She does look sort of familiar."

"Hello," called the little girl suddenly. "My name's Martha. Who are you?" And then Ann knew.

But what she knew seemed so impossible that for a second she couldn't take it in.

"We're caught by cannibals," said the little girl. "Did you come to save us?"

"Yes," said Roger. "I guess we must have. Excuse me a minute." For Ann was tugging at his sleeve.

"Don't you see?" she whispered excitedly. "Didn't you hear her say her name's Martha? It's *Mother!* It's Mother when she was a little girl!"

THE TIME GARDEN

THE TIME GARDEN

EDWARD EAGER

ILLUSTRATED BY
N. M. BODECKER

HOUGHTON MIFFLIN HARCOURT
Boston   New York

First Harcourt Young Classics edition 1999
First Odyssey Classics edition 1990
First published 1958

www.hmhco.com

The Library of Congress has catalogued the hardcover edition as follows:
Eager, Edward.
The time garden/Edward Eager; illustrated by N. M. Bodecker.
p. cm.
Sequel to: Knight's castle.
Summary: While spending the summer in a house by the sea, four cousins,
Roger, Ann, Eliza, and Jack, discover a bank of wild thyme whose magic
propels them on a series of adventures back and forth through time.
[1. Magic—Fiction. 2. Space and time—Fiction. 3. Cousins—Fiction.]
I. Bodecker, N. M., ill. II. Title.
PZ7.E115Ti 1999
[Fic]—dc21 99-22565

ISBN: 978-0-544-67169-0 paperback

Manufactured in the United States of America
DOC 10 9 8 7 6 5 4 3 2 1
4500589297

For Cindy Packard,
a persuasive persuader

Contents

THE TIME GARDEN

1

All the Time in the World

The house and the garden were waiting.

The house had been waiting a long time now, three hundred years, and the garden nearly as long, if you believed Old Henry, who should know. The first garden was planted by the same Robert Whiton who built the house, and it had gone on and on, renewing itself, as gardens do if there are owners who care about them, and the owners of this one did. All the Whitons had green thumbs.

Old Mrs. Whiton, who lived all alone in the house now, didn't, or at least Old Henry said she didn't, but then she was only a Whiton by marriage. She had been born a Miss Peterson, of Passaic, New Jersey. Even though she had lived in the house for over fifty years, Old Henry still considered her a foreigner.

As for the bank of thyme that led down from the garden to the sea, Old Henry said that his grandfather had said that *his* grandfather had said that it had been there when he was a boy.

What the Natterjack would have said, no one could tell, for no one had asked him. The Natterjack did not mind. He bided his time. He could wait.

He and the house and the garden were waiting. They were waiting for four children. They didn't care how long they waited. They had all the time in the world.

Right now the four children were on a train. How they happened to be there is a long story. It is longest for Roger and Ann.

It all started when their father, who had never done anything unusual before, suddenly surprised everybody by writing a play. Of course it was a good play, because everything their father did with his mind was good (though his swings fell down and his rabbit hutches came apart).

And it must have been good, because the first man who read it wanted to put it on the stage right away. Only he wanted to put it on in England first and see how it went, before putting it on in America.

When Ann and Roger heard the news, they were jubilant.

"We can see the Tower of London!" said Roger.

"And Blackheath, where the Bastable children lived!" said Ann.

Their father and mother exchanged a look. It was the kind of look Roger and Ann had seen and grown to know in the past, and it usually meant that something could not be afforded.

"You see," said their father slowly, as though he didn't want to say it, "*we* all like the play, but maybe the audiences won't. And until we know . . ."

"Yes, of course," said Roger.

"We understand," said Ann.

"If it's a big hit, we'll send for you right away, and all have a wonderful time," said their mother.

There was a silence.

"What about the meantime?" said Roger. "Where'll we be?"

"That," said their father, "will take some working out."

"I think," said their mother, "I'll put in a call to Baltimore right now."

"Jack and Eliza?" said Ann, and her eyes danced, for she and Roger had had a wonderful yeomanly magic summer in Baltimore, Maryland, the year before, with the cousins of those names.

"No, Martha," said their father. "We can't go running to your sister Katharine to help us every time we have a problem!"

"I think," said their mother, "I'll put in a call anyway, just in case."

And it turned out it was a lucky thing she did. Because it turned out that Aunt Katharine and Uncle John were planning a trip to England this summer, too, and they'd been wondering what to do about Jack and Eliza.

"It's just a quick business trip," said Aunt Katharine into the phone. "We wouldn't have time to take them places. It wouldn't be fair."

After that the wires buzzed almost every night between Baltimore, Maryland, and Toledo, Ohio (where Ann and Roger lived), as one parent or another had a wonderful new idea about where to send the four children for the summer.

Only for one reason or another all the wonderful ideas fell through.

It was getting to be the middle of May and summer was fast approaching when Aunt Katharine thought of old Mrs. Whiton.

"It's the perfect solution," she said into the phone that night to Ann and Roger's mother. "She's kind of a great-aunt of John's. She lives in a wonderful historic old house on the South Shore near Boston and she loves having children stay with her. She writes children's books or something."

"It'll be ghastly," said Eliza to Jack, when she heard the news. "She'll keep wanting to draw us out. She'll keep wanting to get at the content of the child mind!"

"Really, Eliza," said Aunt Katharine.

"That's enough, Eliza," said Uncle John. And that was that.

And the next thing that happened was June, and school closed its hideous doors, and all was trunks and tickets, and in practically no time Roger and Ann found themselves with their father and mother on the train to New York City.

Roger didn't bring his model soldiers and knights

with him this time, because he had outgrown all that (except for an occasional sliding back now and then, and strictly in private). But he hadn't outgrown some other things, and when Ann looked at him in a certain expectant, excited way, he knew perfectly well what she was thinking, and winked at her across the dining-car table.

What Ann was thinking was that maybe this summer would turn out to be a wonderful magic one like the summer before. It had a lot of magic-seeming things in it already—parents being called away and four children sent to stay in an old house by the sea. Lots of magic adventures in books started out that way.

But the next morning came New York City, which has a magic of its own, and Ann and Roger's first sight of it was enough to blot out all thought of summer adventures, or indeed of anything else.

Jack and Eliza and Aunt Katharine and Uncle John met them in the station and took them back to their hotel, and for the next three days they looked at tall buildings, and battled with shopping crowds, and went round Manhattan Island on a ferryboat, and saw wonderful plays called *Kismet* and *The Pajama Game* and *The Teahouse of the August Moon,* only Roger and

Ann knew all along that their father's play would be even better than any of them.

And then came the day of the sailing, and there was the great steamer to explore, and Eliza was spoken to severely by a man in uniform who might have been the captain, for running and sliding on the floor of the ship's ballroom. And all too soon the ship's whistle thrillingly blew, and there came the age-old cry of "All ashore that's going ashore."

Everybody kissed everybody, and some cried (I will not say which ones), and the four children made their way down the gangplank. Ann stood with sinking heart on the pier and watched the watery gulf grow wider and her mother's smiling face go farther and farther away till she couldn't make it out anymore, but still there were waving hands to be seen, and she waved back at them till at last her arm grew tired and stopped of its own accord.

The four children turned away from the water. Nobody looked at anybody else, and Ann could tell that the others must be having that same sinking feeling, too.

Jack was the first to recover. "Now then," he said importantly. "Find a taxi and go straight to Grand Central Station." For those were the instructions that had been gone over and repeated again and again till all four children could have said them in their sleep.

Grand Central Station turned out to be even more interesting than Ann and Roger had thought when they first arrived there three days before. They and Eliza could have lingered for hours looking at tropical fruit and magazine stands and gentlemen's haberdashery, but Jack would have none of this, hustling them along, finding the right gate and tipping redcaps in a lordly way, till soon Roger and Ann were sitting in their seats in the parlor car, and Eliza was running back and forth looking out of windows and comparing the car unfavorably with others she had ridden in in the past.

This train would take them as far as Boston. Their parents had decided it would be all right for them to go that far alone, because Jack was old enough now to take care of the others.

"Though a lot of care he'll take, if I know him," Eliza had said to Ann. "Not with this new horrible side of him that's beginning to show!"

And sure enough, hardly had they left the station and gone through the tunnel than Jack broke off in the middle of a conversation he was having with

Roger about the Brooklyn Dodgers, and sat staring up the car and across the aisle, his eyes taking on a glazed expression.

What he was staring at was a female form that had just taken its seat halfway up the car. A few seconds later he got up and went into the washroom and slicked down his hair, and came back and sat on the arm of the female form's chair, and started muttering to her in a husky monotone that went up an octave every so often, when his voice broke. Each time this happened, the female form uttered a titter.

"Honestly!" said Eliza to Ann. "To think we'll all come to that some day! If there's one thing I despise, it's a teenage girl!"

"Disgusting," Ann agreed.

"He won't be a bit of use to us all summer, you mark my words!" said Eliza.

Roger's heart sank. What was he going to do with himself in a strange house with just two hapless females and a cousin who liked teenage girls?

When lunchtime came, Jack sat with his new friend, and acted as if he'd never seen the other three before in his life, and sent their lunch money over to them by a waiter.

And when the afternoon had dragged its weary length along, and they pulled into the South Station in Boston, his behavior was even more insulting.

"Well, so long," he said regretfully to the teenage girl. "I have to manage these helpless infants now."

"How too sickening for you," said the teenage girl.

The blood of Ann and Roger and Eliza boiled.

There was a slight delay at the South Station, because no one was quite sure what to do next. Old Mrs. Whiton had written that she would try to have Old Henry meet them, but that he was very difficult, and might refuse.

"He'd better not try being difficult with *me!*" Eliza had muttered darkly, when she heard those words.

But as five minutes passed, and nobody who looked as though he might be called Old Henry came up to them, it seemed that he was trying it.

So then Jack got out old Mrs. Whiton's letter, and read the instructions in it, and found the right platform, and there was the train for the South Shore. Only it wasn't much of a train, being only one car long.

They had to wait quite a while for the train to start. Jack made conversation.

"That was some keen girl," he said. "Her name was Betsy Johnson. She goes to Dana Hall."

"Does she?" said Roger.

By the time the train started, Ann was too sleepy and hungry to care much what was happening, but Roger sat staring interestedly out on the passing New England countryside, and reading the names of the different stations, till it got too dark to see.

As for Eliza, she bounced over to the opposite seat and tried the window to see whether it would open or not, and it did, and after that she hung her head out, sniffing for the first scent of the sea, till the conductor came by and asked if she wanted to get herself killed.

"Ha!" said Eliza. "By a mere train? Not very likely!" But she shut the window.

Their station was the last on the line, and by the time they got there it was almost completely dark. The four children jumped down to the platform and stood looking around.

A figure approached, and a grizzled face regarded them without affection.

"So it's you, is it?" said the figure. There didn't seem to be any answer to this. "Come along then, if that's the way it's going to be," it went on. And it shuffled away into the night without offering to help them with their luggage, and the four children agreed that if difficult was the word for Old Henry, this must be he.

They followed him, lugging the heavy suitcases, and came to what must be the oldest black sedan in the world. Jack, who knew about such things, said it was a Willys-Knight, and they were extinct, and it ought to be in a museum.

Old Henry hardly gave them time to get loaded before he stepped on the gas, and the car slithered away, over smooth highway at first, but then they turned into a woods, over a rocky road that bumped.

And at last the bumping ended and they came out onto cleared land, and there was the house, standing bleak and severe and beautiful, the cold moonlight turning its weathered boards to silver.

Old Henry slithered the car to a stop, and started shuffling off into the night again, but a deep, gruff voice called from the open doorway.

"Come back here and help with those bags, you old ruffian," said the voice. And that was the four children's first introduction to old Mrs. Whiton.

The rest of that evening was a confusion of unpacking and exploring, and abrupt steep staircases,

and long rambling corridors that went up and down sudden unexpected steps and never seemed to lead where you thought they were leading. And always in the background was the boom of the sea, and yet the four children couldn't see it from any of the windows, because it lay far below, at the foot of the cliff on which the house was built, so old Mrs. Whiton told them.

Old Mrs. Whiton didn't talk much or smile much, and what she did say sounded rather grim and forbidding, but that may have been because her voice was so deep. And she didn't try to draw them out or get at the content of the child mind, either.

She gave them a supper of baked beans and hot Boston brown bread, and then she said they would have plenty of time for exploring tomorrow, and now they had better go to bed, because the waves were sure to wake them early, till they got used to them. And she showed the four children to their rooms.

There were two rooms, one for the boys and one for the girls, at the end of a long corridor, with their doors directly facing each other. Both rooms had huge fireplaces at one end, big enough to walk into. Over the fireplace in Jack and Roger's room hung two ancient flintlock guns.

14

"Touch those at your peril," said old Mrs. Whiton.

In Ann and Eliza's room were two immense double four-poster beds, and the beds had canopies over them that were called testers, Mrs. Whiton said.

"Testing. Testing," said Eliza, starting to climb up her canopy to see if it would hold her weight.

"Any more of that," said old Mrs. Whiton, plucking her down, "and you'll rue the day." And she left the room.

"Isn't she an old grenadier?" said Eliza. "I like her!"

Ann didn't answer. She was feeling rather small and lonely. And she felt smaller still when she had undressed and climbed into the middle of her vast bed.

Eliza was at the window, flinging the casements wide and peering out. And at last she saw the sea, curling whitely on the rocks below. A thrill went through her. "This," she announced, "is a wonderful house. Spies could land here, and nobody'd ever know. Smugglers probably used it, in the olden days. It's probably honeycombed with secret passages. Indians could come down through the woods and slaughter everybody!"

There was no answer from Ann's bed. Ann was asleep.

Eliza wandered across the corridor and paused

at the door of Jack and Roger's room. Through the door she could hear Jack's voice, telling Roger all about a keen girl he knew called Susan Snook. Roger wasn't answering.

Eliza gave a sniff of disdain, and wandered back to her own room. And standing at the window again, she swore a vow to herself.

"I vow," she swore, "that I'll be the first one up tomorrow and really explore this whole place. *Anything* could happen here!" And she got into bed and turned out the light.

But it was Ann who woke up first the next morning.

She woke up and got dressed quietly and went downstairs, losing her way several times. In the big front hall she met old Mrs. Whiton. Old Mrs. Whiton was wearing an old-fashioned bathing dress that ought to have looked very funny, but somehow on old Mrs. Whiton it didn't.

"So it's you, is it?" she said. "Get your bathing things and follow me."

Ann ran back for her bathing things, still not waking Eliza, and followed Mrs. Whiton. They went down, not through the garden, but by a hidden flight of steps, cut in the face of the cliff.

"My ancestors built this stairway," said old Mrs. Whiton. "Stone by stone."

At the foot of the stairway was a tiny beach. The morning was bright and sunny, but there was a wind, and the waves that pounded on the sand were big ones. Ann hung back, but old Mrs. Whiton did not. She plunged boldly in, and after a bit Ann followed. Once the first cold shock was past, the waves were glorious, and the salt taste and the tingling. Ann could have stayed for hours at least, but such was not the order of the day.

"Breakfast now," said old Mrs. Whiton in her deep voice, after what seemed like only a few seconds had passed. She strode up the beach toward the stone steps, and Ann could only follow.

In the hall they met Eliza, in bathrobe and slippers.

"Wretch," she said to Ann. "How dare you get there before me? Wait a minute and I'll fetch my things and we'll go in together."

"You will not," said old Mrs. Whiton. "Breakfast is in five minutes. See that you appear properly dressed. And wake those slothful boys. Tardiness will *not* be excused." And she stalked away in the direction of her ground-floor bedroom.

17

Eliza made a face behind her back, but she obeyed. Five minutes later all four children were scrubbed and neatly dressed and at the table, which goes to show the power of a strong mind.

Breakfast was served by an elderly maid called Mrs. Annable, who seemed to be a maid of few words. She did not smile or speak when the four children were introduced. But the breakfast was hearty and delicious, with applesauce and toasted cornbread and cocoa, and oatmeal that was properly stiff and porridgey.

"No quick-cooking messes," said old Mrs. Whiton. "Inventions of the devil!"

"Not in *my* kitchen!" said Mrs. Annable. "Nor none of your nasty frozen vegetables, neither!" Which was her one remark of the morning.

"And *now,*" said Eliza, when the last crumb had been eaten, and the last drop of buttery cream scraped from the bottom of the last porridge-bowl, "the open sea calls."

"It may call in vain for the next hour and a half," said old Mrs. Whiton. "No one has had cramps and drowned at this beach yet, and I don't intend one of you to be the first!"

Four faces fell. Naturally Eliza was the first to

say what all the others were thinking. "But we can't *wait!*" she said.

"Oh, I think you can," said old Mrs. Whiton. "You've all the time in the world." She started for her room, but in the doorway she seemed to relent a little, and turned. "You can go into the garden while you're waiting," she said. "You *may* find something to interest you." And she stalked away. A few seconds later the click of a typewriter was heard.

"Whatever those books are that she writes," said Roger, "they must be for Spartan children."

"The garden!" said Eliza, in tones of contempt. "What are we supposed to do, make daisy chains?"

But when the four children wandered willy-nilly out into the sun and through an opening in a box-wood hedge, Ann caught her breath, and Jack wished he had brought his color camera, and even Eliza admitted that it wasn't so dusty.

The garden was long and rectangular, and every bloom of June brightened its borders. Fragrance hung on the air, birds sang, and from somewhere nearby came a drowsy, humming sound.

"The murmur of innumerable bees," said Ann, who was liking poetry and big words that year.

"Though I don't see any immemorial elms," said

Roger, who was the family nature-lover. "That's a copper beech." He pointed to the end of the garden.

Beyond the copper beech was another opening in the boxwood hedge. And in the opening stood a sundial.

"Look," said Ann, going closer. "There's something written on it, down at the bottom."

"Don't bother," said Eliza. "It'll just say 'It is later than you think.' They always do."

"If they don't say 'I count only the sunny hours,'" said Jack.

But Ann and Roger had never seen a real sundial before, and Ann had to be shown how it worked, and Roger, who had read all about sundials in a book, showed her. Then they bent over the base of the pedestal. The lettering was old and crumbly and hard to read, but Roger finally made it out.

"It says . . ." He broke off and looked at the others. "It says 'Anything Can Happen!'"

"That isn't all," said Ann, who had wandered around to the back of the sundial. "The lettering goes on, around here. It says . . ." She leaned over to make out the final words. "It says, 'Anything Can Happen When You've All the Time in the World!'"

"What did I tell you?" Eliza's eyes were glowing

now. "That old Mrs. Whiton sent us here on purpose! She's probably a witch! It all connects! It's true! I feel it in my bones! Anything *could* happen here! Something probably *will* any minute!"

As she spoke something flashed through the air and disappeared in the grass at their feet.

"What was that?" said Ann.

"It came from the sundial," said Roger. "Something live must have been sitting there, and then it hopped off."

"There it goes!" said Jack, pointing through the opening in the hedge.

"Come on!" said Eliza.

The four children raced through the opening after the hopping thing. Then they stopped short.

From where they stood a bank led down to the sea, and the bank was all covered with little flat creeping plants that flowed over rock ledges and turned boulders to flowery cushions, for the plants were studded all over with tiny starry blossoms, purple and lavender and white. The smell of the bank was like all the sweetness and spice of the world mixed together. And it was here that the innumerable bees hummed.

The thing they were following gave another hop and landed just ahead of them. "*There* it is!" said Ann.

"Never mind, it's just an old toad," said Eliza. "What's all this wonderful smelly stuff?" And she threw herself down on its redolent pillowiness, and the others followed her example.

"It smells like turkey stuffing," said Jack.

"It's some kind of herb," said Roger. He tasted one of the tiny dark green leaves of the purple-flowering kind. "I think maybe it's thyme."

"You mean it's a bank whereon the wild thyme grows?" said Ann. "That's Shakespeare."

"That's silly," said Eliza, who was not a botanical girl, nor a poetical one, either. "Time doesn't grow. Time flies."

"Not this kind of thyme," said Roger.

"Thyme with an 'h,' " said Jack.

"T, h, y, m, e," said Ann.

"The 'h' is silent," said a fifth voice, "as in 'ospital, 'awthorn and 'edge'og."

The four children looked at each other.

"Who said that?" said Jack.

The hopping thing they had been chasing hopped nearer. "I did," it said. "You see," it went on, "anything *can* 'appen, when you've all the thyme in the world!" And staring at the four children, it slowly winked one eye.

2

Wild Time

The four children stared at the toad (if it *was* a toad).

"You're magic," said Eliza.

"Among other things," said the creature (whatever it was).

"That's funny," said Ann.

"Not necessarily," said the creature, in rather a huffy voice.

"I just meant," Ann went on quickly, "I've never met any magic toads before. We've met magic knights, and castles, but never any toads. Of course there's the *Wind in the Willows* one, but he wasn't magic exactly . . ."

"I should think *not!*" said the creature. "A mere h'upstart of a common or garden toad. *I,*" it announced proudly, puffing itself out, "am a Natterjack."

"What's *that?*" said Jack.

"It's what *I* am, and it's a 'ighly superior thing to be," said the Natterjack.

"You talk sort of British," said Roger.

"And why not?" said the Natterjack. "London born an' London bred my granddaddy's granddaddy was. Served 'is apprenticeship in Covent Garden Flower Market. H'emigrated 'ere on a sod o' primroses, 'e did, an' 'im an' 'is descendants 'ave been tending this 'ere garding ever since. Why d'you suppose the posies 'ere bloom prettier 'n elsewhere? Madam may say it's fertilizer and Old 'Enry may say it's deep trenching, but *I* say it's Natterjacks!" And sticking out its tongue, it consumed a nearby aphid.

The four children waited in respectful silence for the Natterjack to go on. "Well?" prompted Eliza, after a bit. "What else do you do?"

"Eh?' said the Natterjack.

"Where do *we* come in?" said Eliza. "Do you

grant our wishes, or what? You must be going to do *something* for us, or you wouldn't have appeared. It stands to reason."

The Natterjack eyed her very much as it had eyed the aphid. "Some people round 'ere," it said, "are so sharp they'll cut theirselves. Grantin' wishes at *my* time of life, not very likely! Any magic as I 'ave, I puts right into this 'ere garding. Which speakin' o' which, if some people was 'alf so smart as what they thinks they is, when I said the 'h' was silent, they'd 'ave thunk that one through a few times!"

Eliza stared blankly. But Roger began to think he saw light.

"You mean," he said excitedly, "that this really is a *time* garden? The clock kind of time?"

"Time's time, so far as *I* ever 'eard," said the Natterjack. "Some may spell it 'h' and some may spell it 'y,' but *I* spells it not at all, not 'avin' the ed-dycation. *I* just magics it!"

"You mean," said Roger again, "that you put all your magic into the garden? Does that mean that now *it*'s got the magic power?"

The Natterjack gave a hop. It landed on a flow-ery patch that was taller and weedier than the rest, and with pale lilac flowers. "If you was to pluck a sprig o' this 'ere," it said, "an' rub it once an' sniff the breathin' essence of it, I wouldn't say what'd 'appen, but it wouldn't be uninterestin'. An' I wouldn't say *when* the time'd be, but it wouldn't be *now!*"

Roger and Ann and Eliza looked at each other with gleaming eyes. Jack chose this moment to act his age.

"This is silly," he said. "I don't believe it. I'm going back to the house."

The other three were aghast.

"Don't you *want* an adventure?" said Eliza. "Don't you want to tour round olden times and alter history?"

"Don't you remember last summer," said Roger, "and the Giants' Lair, and Robin Hood?"

Jack looked tempted. Then he looked stubborn. "Kid stuff," he said. "We probably just dreamed the whole thing. That toad isn't talking now. We just think it is. I'm going back to the house. I have to write a letter to Annie Strong." And he walked away.

"Let him go," said Eliza. "It'll mean that much more magic for the rest of us! Come on!" And she reached out for the patch of thyme where the

Natterjack was sitting, and grabbed so eagerly that a whole rooted tuft came away in her hand.

"'Ere, 'ere, not so greedy!" said the Natterjack, in what Ann thought sounded like tones of alarm. "A sprig would 'ave been h'ample!"

But it was too late. Eliza was rubbing the whole tuft between her hands, and now she held them out, and she and Roger and Ann leaned over them and drew the spicy scent deep into their lungs. Then they straightened up and looked around.

Nothing seemed to have changed. The house was still the same, and so was the garden. And they didn't seem to be in olden times, because Roger was still wearing his patched blue jeans, and Eliza her blue school jumper and Ann her old pink dress with the smocking.

It was Ann who noticed the different thing first.

"Look!" she cried. "It's the sun. It's moved. It used to be over there."

The others looked where she pointed. Sure enough, the sun had changed position and was sinking toward the horizon in a red and yellow glow. Its last long rays touched the house and gilded it for a moment before it set completely.

"What a hoax!" said Eliza. "All we did was change the time from morning to evening! Now we've lost a whole day out of our lives, and I never did get to have that first swim!"

As she spoke, the last afterglow faded, and it began growing dark fast.

"Wait," said Roger. "There must be more to it than that."

The three children looked around again. This time it was Eliza who saw the odd thing first. The others didn't see it till a second later.

The odd thing was a shape, just out to sea, that was darker than the rest of the dark around it. The shape was the shape of a large boat or a small ship, with a single sail.

"A skiff," muttered Eliza, "or a small sloop. We're back in sailing-boat days!"

"Maybe not," said Roger. "Maybe it's just the South Shore Yacht Club."

"Without a light showing?" scoffed Eliza. "Not very likely! We're in olden times, I tell you! It's spies! Or smugglers! Or both!"

Now as they watched, a ship's lantern did suddenly show against the dark, and then another. The skiff (or sloop) was signaling.

"'One if by land and two if by sea!'" counted Ann. "Maybe it's *that* olden time."

"It couldn't be," said Roger. "That's Paul Revere. That's Boston and Lexington and Concord, not the South Shore!"

"Oh, that old Paul Revere!" said Eliza. "Do you suppose he got to have all the fun? Don't you suppose anybody else got to help spread the news, too? Hark!"

Everybody harked. There was a sound in the night. And though none of the three children had ever heard that exact sound before, all agreed that it could only be muffled oars! A few seconds later, a prow ground on sand and there came a cautious footfall on the secret stairway in the rock. A light issued forth from a door somewhere in the back of the house, and there was a sound of low voices.

"Dark deeds," muttered Eliza, "and secret meetings by moonlight. What could be sweeter? Come on. Let's lurk. We're missing it all. Let's deploy about the building."

"Let's not," said Ann.

But at that moment the light grew nearer and brighter, and the figure of a woman appeared, silhouetted against the house, a lantern in her hand.

"Prudence! Deborah! Preserved!" she called.

"Who's she talking to?" hissed Eliza.

"I think . . ." said Ann, timidly. "I think maybe she means us. I think maybe she thinks we're her children."

And it seemed that the woman did, for now she had seen them and was beckoning.

"Where do you suppose the real Prudence and the rest of them are?" wondered Roger.

"Who knows? Probably back in *our* time, scaring the populace," said Eliza. "Come on."

She ran forward, eager for whatever was to come, and Roger followed her. Ann tagged along behind, with dubious heart. As she drew near the light, she noticed a small form, hopping along in the grass beside her, and a voice sounded.

"That's gratitude for you," it said. "Off to your fun an' games with never a 'int of a thank you or a 'elping 'and for me, not that *I* mind, I'm sure! *I'm* not one to push myself in where I'm not h'asked!"

"But I *am* asking you!" said Ann. "Won't you come along? I'd really rather you did." And she meant it. Because if this were going to be a scary adventure, it might be just as well to have a magic being within call. So she put down a helping hand, and the Natterjack hopped on, and Ann stowed it carefully in her pocket, before running into the house after the others.

The woman was waiting in the hall. "Come. Quickly," she said, leading the way toward the back of the house.

"She didn't notice a thing," whispered Roger to Eliza. "Not our modern clothes, or being different, or anything."

"Probably she didn't see them," whispered Eliza. "Probably to her we're all in olden costume. Linsey-woolsey and stuff like that."

They followed the woman into the kitchen, and even though Roger was sure by now they'd gone back to olden times, or just about, the room looked almost the same to him as when he'd had breakfast there that morning. Except that in some ways it was different, being seemingly used as kitchen and living room combined.

A great fire roared in the chimney, and pacing up and down before the hearth was a gentleman in a greatcoat who must be the person who had just arrived in the boat. On a settle by the fire was another gentleman, with a quilt over his knees and a red flannel bandage round his throat.

"Children," said the woman, "here is Mr. Frothingham arrived from Boston with dreadful news. The Redcoats are coming!"

"Brave men will ride tonight!" said the gentleman in the greatcoat, pacing faster. "Tell the countryside! Rouse every South Shore village and town!"

"Naturally," said Eliza.

"We thought that must be it," said Roger.

The gentleman looked surprised and impressed at their coolness.

"And here is your father ill with the quinsy and unable to venture from the house," said the woman.

The other gentleman, the one with the bandage, smiled at Roger and put a hand on his shoulder. "But my son Preserved here has a fine pair of hands with a horse, ay, and a good strong voice, also, and may more than fitly fill my place," he said.

Roger, who had seldom been on a horse in his life, gulped, and tried to look ready for anything.

"What about me?" said Eliza. "Haven't I just as good hands as he has?"

"Prudence, Prudence," said the woman. "Must you ever belie your name?"

"If the others are going, I want to go, too!" said Ann, suddenly. She was just as surprised as everyone else was to find herself saying it.

"Nay, Deborah!" cried the woman. "You are too young for such charades!"

But the gentleman in the greatcoat smote his thigh in a dashing and hot-blooded way. "By thunder!" he cried. "If the youngest Yankee of them all is not afraid to ride for liberty, then surely the right will prevail. To horse, and quickly!"

"The groom is readying the steeds now," said the father of Preserved and Prudence and Deborah. There seemed to be a twinkle in his eye. Even as he spoke, a thudding of hoofs was heard from without.

"Deary me, pray that no harm befall you! Preserved, do not forget your muffler. Girls, your mittens and tippets!" cried the woman, fussing around the three children and buttoning them up, as mothers always will, whatever the century.

They went out into the stable yard, all but the bandaged gentleman, who remained watching from a window, out of regard for his quinsy.

Ann and Roger were relieved when the steeds turned out to be an elderly roan for the gentleman and a trio of dapple-gray ponies for the three younger ones, but Eliza was scornful. She had hoped for a wild Arabian stallion, at *least*.

Good-byes were said, and the mother of Preserved and Prudence and Deborah kissed Roger and Eliza and Ann (and didn't seem to sense any difference, though Ann had always heard a mother could *tell!*) and the four riders took the road.

Ann was pleased to discover, after a few minutes, that she could ride quite well. She even began to enjoy it. It must be the Deborah in her, she decided. Then she thought of the Natterjack, and wondered if he were smothering under the fur-lined cloak the mother of Deborah had buttoned round her, or if the motion were making him seasick. But she couldn't get at her pocket to see.

It was twelve by Roger's new wristwatch as they came out of the woods onto the main road, because he looked, and decided his watch must be a really good one, to keep pace with the sudden way time had been changing.

"Paul Revere's just crossing the bridge into Medford town now," he remarked.

The man in the greatcoat threw him a surprised look. "You seem to know all about it!" he said. "Our counterespionage system must be doing well in these parts."

"I was just quoting Henry Wadsworth Longfellow," said Roger.

"I don't know the gentleman," said the man. "But if he is a Son of Liberty, more power to him!"

A mile or so beyond the turning, the road forked, and a huddle of dark houses could be seen up ahead in either direction. The gentleman in the greatcoat slowed his horse.

"You take the high road," he said, "and I'll take the other. Knock at every door. Tell all brave men we meet by the rude bridge that arched the flood. Don't let Lexington and Concord do it all!"

He galloped away to the left, and the three children pressed forward, on the right-hand road. At the first house they reined in.

"Well?" said Ann.

"Come on!" said Eliza. "Not that it makes any difference. The minutemen won, anyway."

"You never can tell," said Roger. "Maybe the real Deborah and Prudence and Preserved *did* ride that night. Maybe if they hadn't, not as many minutemen would have been ready and the whole war might have ended differently. At least we're doing our bit!" And he jumped from his pony and ran to give a loud knock on the door.

The man who appeared at a window (after the third knock) had his nightcap on, and was not pleased at being disturbed. But when he heard the news, he ran to load his musket, and dress, and head north to join the patriot troops.

It was the same at the second house. And at the third, the man had three strong grown-up sons who would march with him.

"That makes six extra minutemen so far that might not have got there if it weren't for us," said Roger, in satisfied tones.

"Why don't we run into any Tories or traitors?" said Eliza. "This is getting monotonous."

They were riding along a stretch of highway with no houses now, but in the distance another building showed, this one with lights at the windows, in spite of the late hour. As the three children rode up to it, they saw that it was a wayside inn. But it did not look like one that would have been recommended by Mr. Duncan Hines, if he had been alive in those days. Its aspect was ramshackle and its garden overgrown. Its windows were dirty. Over its doorway a sign clanked on rusty chains. The sign read, "The Hanged Man." From within came a sound of raucous voices raised in ribald song.

"We don't have to go in *there,* do we?" said Ann.

"Of course. This is the best part yet!" cried Eliza, jumping down from her pony. "Follow me."

So of course they had to.

The ribald song broke off as Eliza made her dramatic entrance into the taproom of the inn, followed, less dramatically, by Ann and Roger. A dozen evil-looking fellows sat hunched over mugs of grog, served by a bold-faced lady who stood behind the bar.

"To arms!" announced Eliza, in thrilling tones. "The British are attacking!"

"What? Where?" cried most of the men, running to the windows to peer out into the darkness.

"They're not here yet," said Roger. "They're stopping at Lexington first."

"Oh. Why didn't you say so? Let *them* take care of it, then," said nearly everybody, sitting down again and calling for more grog.

Eliza's dander rose.

"Shame on you," she cried. "What does it matter where they attack first? Aren't we all in this together? Aren't we the United States of America?"

A burly, dark-browed man put down his mug with a scowl (and a thump). "No!" he said. "No, we ain't! And if you ask me, we're not going to be! Once we're free of the pesky British, it's every man for himself, *I* say!"

"Why," cried Eliza, in tones of outrage, "that's anarchy!"

"None of your big words!" growled the man, peering at her suspiciously. "Who be you, anyway?"

"'Tis Master Whiton's children, from the great house on the cliff," put in the bold-faced woman, from behind the bar.

"Ay, that Master Whiton," cried another of the men. "He be ever stirrin' up trouble with his radical talk o' unions!"

"Sooner should he keep his brats safe home abed o' nights, 'stead o' wanderin' the highway preachin' seditious talk!" muttered a third man.

The black-browed man lurched to his feet. "To the devil with your Master Whiton!" he cried. "To the devil with your United States of America! What's Connecticut to me or me to Connecticut? Nay, or New York, neither? To the devil with all thrones, dominations an' princely powers! To the devil with the Continental Congress!"

38

And all the men drank to this and pounded their mugs on the tables.

Even the mild-natured Ann was provoked to wrath. "Why, you nasty things!" she cried. "What are you, pro–British?"

"No," said the black-browed one, "we ain't. We ain't pro-anything. To the devil with King George, too!" And he and all the men drank again.

Ann had put back her cloak, in the warm air of the inn (and the warm glow of anger), and the noise of the pounding mugs had waked the Natterjack, which had been lulled to sleep by the rhythm of the ride. Now it sat up and began to take notice. It peered out of Ann's pocket just in time to hear these last words, and its British blood boiled.

"Rule, Britannia!" it shrilled suddenly. "Merrie England forever! Britons never, never, never shall be slaves!"

There was a silence.

"Who said that?" said the scowling, black-browed man.

Everybody looked at Roger and Eliza and Ann. One or two rude ones pointed.

The black-browed man moved menacingly over to the three children and stood glaring down at them.

"Aha!" he said. "I see it all now. These brats are spies, ay, and their fine-talking pa, too, always pratin' o' liberty an' union! And all the while the deepest-dyed traitor of them all! Sendin' these young limbs to distract us with false reports an' lead us astray while the Redcoats attack an' burn our houses an' our wives and children!"

"No, we're not! Honest!" said Roger.

"He confesses it!" cried the man, mishearing Roger's words on purpose. "'No, we are not honest' he cries, and there was never a truer word spoke! Away with them to their own house and burn *it* to the ground for a nest of Tory turncoats!"

"No, don't do that!" cried Ann, thinking of the kind mother and the nice man with the bandage.

"Don't worry," muttered Roger. "The house didn't really burn. It's still standing."

"That doesn't signify. Maybe somebody built it up again, afterwards," muttered Eliza.

A ring of hostile faces surrounded the three children. But Roger squared up to them spunkily.

"You make me sick," he cried. "You wouldn't fight when you could be a help, oh no. But when it's a question of picking on innocent people, you're all patriotic all of a sudden!"

41

"Stow your gab!" cried the black-browed man. "And speak the truth. *Are* the Redcoats attacking? And *if* they are, where?"

"We told you," said Roger, stoutly. "We *did* speak the truth."

"We're not spies. We're American patriots," said Eliza.

The Natterjack chose this moment to sing "The British Grenadiers."

"You hear?" said the black-browed man. "The bigger ones brazen it out, but the small one gives them away!"

"I didn't!" said Ann, indignantly.

"That wasn't her, that was *him!*" cried Eliza, desperation taking the place of grammar. She pointed.

"Oh, to be in h'England," remarked the Natterjack, "now that April's 'ere."

The people looked where Eliza was pointing. They saw the toadlike creature teetering on the edge of Ann's pocket, and fell back in horror. The black-browed man was the first to recover.

"'Tis witchcraft!" he cried. "See the small witch with her familiar by her side? This be worse than ever! To the ducking-pond with them!"

"Nay!" said another. "Roasting be the best cure

for witches! To their house, and roast the whole witch family!"

"Why not both?" said the black-browed man. "Duck first and roast afterwards!" And this suggestion proved popular with the crowd.

A dozen hands seized Roger and Eliza and Ann and hustled them through the door. Outside the April wind blew chill.

"You can swim, can't you?" called Eliza to Ann, as they were borne along.

"Just dog paddle," admitted Ann, trying to sound brave.

The pond was beyond the stable yard, lying cold and dank and dark under the steely stars. Ann's teeth chattered to look at it.

"Now then," said the black-browed one. "Up with them and swing them out over it, with a one, two, and three. On the third swing let go. If they be witches, the devil will help them swim and they can be dried off and roasted. If they are not witches but just spies, they may sink and good riddance!"

"One!" And Eliza and Roger and Ann swung out on the chilly air.

"Two!" Again they went swinging over the murky depths.

And it was then, as all breath failed, that the next thing happened.

A war whoop sounded from the wooded hills all around, and a hundred savage painted Indians ran howling down upon the inn yard. Those who were holding Roger and Ann and Eliza dropped them, fortunately upon dry land.

The three children huddled in each other's arms and watched the scene of carnage that followed.

Tomahawks sliced and arrows whirred. Scalps were lost. Blood flowed. From the first, the white men were hopelessly outnumbered.

"Good. There goes that mean one," said Eliza, as the black-browed man toppled to the ground.

Roger and Ann were not so pleased.

"This is awful," said Ann, covering her eyes.

"Don't worry. It didn't happen," Roger comforted her. "Not really. History would have mentioned it."

"Then *we* must have done it," said Ann. "We came back through time and made history *worse!*"

Eliza was more practical. A horrid thought had suddenly occurred to her. "What happens when they kill all the rest?" she said. "Then do they toma-hawk *us?*" She turned to the Natterjack, where it still crouched on the edge of Ann's pocket. "Can't you *do* something? How do we get out of here?"

"The same way you got h'in," said the Natterjack calmly. "I trust you still 'ave plenty of thyme?"

Eliza scrabbled among her clothes. At first she couldn't find the lilac-flowered plant. Then, just as the last whiteskin bit the dust and the Indians circled howling around the three children, she located it, where she'd thrust it down in the bottom of her jumper pocket.

"Quick. Take a big whiff," said the Natterjack. And the three children did.

A second later the tumult and the shouting died, and they found themselves once more sitting on a flowery bank by the sea, on a sunny June morning in modern times.

"Whew!" said Ann.

"That," said Eliza, "is putting it mildly."

"It was all going fine for a while," said Roger. "Then it got crazy."

Eliza glared at the Natterjack. "Really!" she said. "Some creatures!"

The Natterjack gave an embarrassed cough. "Ahem," it said. "I'm afraid I forgot myself there for a moment. But their talk was more than flesh and blood could stand. After all . . ." and it puffed itself out proudly, "h'I'm a Briton! Besides," it added, with a severe look at Eliza, "I warned you not to be greedy. Wasting thyme never pays. Better put that plant back while you still can."

The tuft that was clutched in Eliza's hand looked pretty grubby by now, what with all it had been through, but when she poked it back into the earth, it seemed to perk up and grow again, and looked as good as new.

"That's better," said the Natterjack. "Dangerous thing to leave lying about, thyme is. Specially that sort there. That there is *wild* thyme."

"No wonder," said Roger.

"It was wild all right," said Eliza.

"How many kinds of time are there?" said Ann.

"As many as you'll find in the garden catalog," said the Natterjack. "And now," it added with a yawn, "it's nap time." And it shut its eyes and would say no more, no matter how hard Eliza poked it.

Ann got up and started away purposefully. The others followed. She went right around the house to Old Henry's potting shed.

Old Henry looked up from a tray of Canterbury bell seedlings and eyed the three children coldly.

"Please," said Ann, "may we borrow your garden catalog?"

"And what put that idea into your head?" said Old Henry, suspiciously. "No messing about with my borders, mind!"

"Oh no," Ann assured him. "I just want to look up about the different kinds of thyme."

All three children thought they saw a change come over Old Henry's grim countenance, almost as though he were pleased at something, though that could hardly be.

"Oho," he said. "So that's the way it is, is it? Look your fill, then. But no mucking about the garden with it and leaving it out in the rain, now!"

"We won't," said Ann. "We'll look at it right here." And sitting down on the doorstep, she opened the book and found the place among the T's.

"For heaven's sake! There's a whole page of them!" said Eliza, bending to read over Ann's shoulder and breathing down her neck.

"Thymus serpyllum," Ann read slowly from the list, stumbling over the big word. "Creeping thyme."

"What's that supposed to do, turn us back into mere creeping babes?" said Eliza. "No, thanks."

"There's lots more kinds," said Ann, her eyes traveling down the page. "Silver thyme and golden thyme and lemon thyme and woolly thyme and . . ."

There was an interruption. Old Mrs. Whiton appeared on the path. She was wearing her old-fashioned bathing dress again. Following her was Jack, wearing *his* bathing suit.

"Come along, children," said old Mrs. Whiton. "It's swimming time."

3

Time Will Tell

"I keep worrying," said Ann.

"What about?" said Eliza.

The four children were lying on the beach, after their swim. Old Mrs. Whiton had gone back to the house, leaving strict instructions that the others weren't to lounge about in their wet bathing suits for a minute more than half an hour.

"I keep worrying about those poor people at that inn," said Ann, "after those Indians got them."

"Serves them right, if you ask me," said Eliza.

"But it was our fault," said Ann. "And they may

have been mean, but they didn't deserve to be massacred."

"Maybe they weren't," said Roger. "Maybe after we disappeared the time jumped back, and everything was just as though it had never happened. Sometimes magic works like that."

"Sometimes it doesn't," said Ann. "Remember last summer? Every single thing we did counted. Think back."

Everybody thought back except Jack, who didn't seem to want to.

"Honestly!" he said. "Can't you talk about anything else? Anyway, it didn't happen. You just dreamed it. All that stuffing-y smell put you to sleep."

"We wouldn't all dream the same dream, silly," said Eliza.

"Sure you would. It happens all the time. Look at flying saucers! Mass hypnosis, it's called."

Roger shook his head. "This was real, all right."

"Rave on!" said Jack. He got up. "I just thought. There was this girl that came to visit, back home. Gretsie Kroll, her name was. She came from up around here somewhere. Maybe if I look in the phone book I can find her number." And he started climbing the rock stair to the house.

"What did I tell you?" said Eliza. "It's the end of a noble mind. He's lost to us."

There was a pause.

"I still keep worrying," said Ann. She got to her feet. "I'm going to ask the Natterjack. *He'd* know."

She started up the steps and the others followed. They went past the house and into the garden. The Natterjack lay dormant upon the sundial. But when the three children came near, it woke up and jumped down and started hopping away as fast as it could.

It was Eliza who caught it, with a flying tackle.

"Oh no you don't," it said. "No more tricks today. The garden wouldn't stand it. It'd wilt."

"Oh, I *know*," said Ann. "So would *we!*"

"We don't want any more magic for ages," said Roger.

"Not till tomorrow, at *least!*" said Eliza.

"We have to think," said Roger, "and plan, first."

"We've been thinking *now*," said Ann. "And I've been wondering. About those people."

And she told the Natterjack her worries about the Indian massacre.

The Natterjack was silent in thought. Then it spoke. "I 'ave 'eard," it said, "that the h'evil that men do lives after them . . ."

"'The good is oft interred with their bones,'" Ann finished the quotation. Then a look of horror came over her face. "Do you mean the bad things we do last, and the good ones *don't?*"

"That wouldn't be fair," said Roger.

"It would be just like that magic, though," said Eliza, "always thwarting us!"

"I was thinking," said the Natterjack, "more the other way round."

"You mean . . . ?" Roger puzzled it out. "You mean the mistakes we make come out of the adventure with us, and don't do any harm, but the good things we do stay buried in the past, and turn real?"

"That," said the Natterjack, "is the general h'idea."

"But that makes it dandy," said Eliza. "We can go biffing and banging around to our heart's content, and no harm done to anybody!"

The Natterjack eyed her coldly. "I 'ave also 'eard," it said, "that one good turn deserves another."

The three children thought about this.

"You mean," said Roger again, "that unless we do a good deed in each adventure, we don't get another one?"

"That's fair enough, isn't it?" said the Natterjack.

"What good deed did we do this time?" said Ann.

"If any," said Eliza.

"We got six extra minutemen," Roger reminded them. "Would that count?"

"Under the circumstances," said the Natterjack, "I would say that it was h'almost h'adequate." And it seemed to smile as it digested a passing midge.

"Good," said Eliza. "Then we can go on and on, the whole summer. How long does the magic last?"

"Till the thyme is ripe," said the Natterjack. It hopped away. Then it changed its mind and hopped back again.

"One other thing," it said. "I'm 'ere to mind this 'ere garding, and you're 'ere to mind *me*. Try any tricks when I'm not looking, and beware!"

"We won't," said Roger.

"We'll be good," said Ann.

Eliza nodded in agreement, but Ann saw her cross two fingers of one hand, behind her back. "When do we get our next chance?" she asked.

"Time will tell," said the Natterjack. And it gave an extra-long leap and landed on a cushion of purple blossoms, and promptly went to sleep.

"Look at it," said Eliza, enviously. "It's probably ages away, back in purple time by now, whenever that would be."

"Probably the Roman Empire," said Roger. "The Emperors were born to the purple, weren't they?"

"If we were there with it," said Eliza, "we could rescue a martyr from a lion. That'd be a really good deed."

"I'm glad we're not," said Ann. "I don't feel like lions today."

"Anyway, we'd probably do something wrong," said Roger. "Probably make Rome decline and fall sooner than it would have, even. We've got to plan better for next time."

"Yes," said Eliza, "only not now. We've the whole South Shore to explore."

And for the next few days the three children did just that, learning to dig for clams and learning to like the taste of them after they had been dug (and fried), swimming and looking for seashells and cast-up treasure and then swimming again. One night was the Fourth of July and they saw a fireworks display in a nearby town, and on another night they went to a wonderful place called Nantasket where there were roller coasters and Ferris wheels. Old Mrs. Whiton on the roller coaster was terrible and wonderful to behold.

Sometimes Jack was with the other three, but

mostly he wasn't. Because, even though he hadn't found Gretsie Kroll in the phone book, he had met two teenage girls on the roller coaster called Barbara Granbery and Joan Chapin, and after that when he wasn't on the phone he was mostly hitchhiking to

the house of one or the other. Eliza and Roger and Ann despaired of him, but old Mrs. Whiton said he was going through a phase.

And so the days went by, full of happy events and marine life. But no day is too full for the thought of magic to creep in now and again, and once Roger stole off to the garden by himself and found Ann already there looking for the Natterjack (only it wasn't to be seen), and on another day Eliza and Ann and Roger all met by chance and at once on the fragrant blossomy bank. The scent of thyme hung in the air, but the Natterjack was conspicuous by its absence.

"Time will tell!" snorted Eliza disgustedly, as they trailed back past the sundial into the main garden. "Only it never says a thing!"

Ann sat down on a stone bench. She had absently picked a sprig of thyme blossom from the bank. Now she held it to her ear.

"What good do you think *that*'ll do?" said Eliza, jigging restlessly up and down the borders. "Do you think a dear little fairy's going to peek out of a flower bell and talk to you? More likely a dear little bee!" She gazed across the garden. "What's Roger supposed to be doing?"

Ann looked. So far as she could see, Roger wasn't doing anything, just standing and staring at the sundial. Now he spoke. "Come here," he said, and there was something in his voice that made Eliza and Ann go there right away.

He pointed at the sundial. "Look," he said. "It isn't working!"

"Sure it is. You just can't see it," said Eliza. "It's like trying to watch a tree grow."

"Or a watched pot," said Ann.

"No, honest, it hasn't moved," said Roger, who was a noticing kind of boy. "The shadow's exactly where it was when I went by here this morning. It ought to be way over there by now." He pointed. "It must be stuck or something."

Eliza clutched Ann's arm excitedly. "No! Don't you see what this means? It means time's standing still! And you know what *that* means! It means it's trying to tell us something! Time will tell!"

"Well!" said the Natterjack, appearing suddenly in the grass at their side. "I wondered when light would dawn."

Eliza wasted no time in greetings. "Do you mean to say it's been standing like that for days, waiting for us to notice?" she said. "Of all the mean tricks!"

"Not that we're not grateful," put in Roger quickly, but Eliza had small regard for the niceties.

"What happens next? What time will it be when it starts again? Where'll we go?" she was saying. "Oh, and we meant to plan it all out beforehand and we never did! Never mind, we'll plan now. Now *I* think . . ."

"Wait a bit, wait a bit," said the Natterjack. "Take your time. Oh, I see you already 'ave." It had noticed the sprig of thyme in Ann's hand. Now Ann held it closer so the Natterjack could take a good look.

"But we don't know if it's the right kind!" said Eliza. "We haven't decided a thing!"

The Natterjack eyed the tuft of thyme with its crimson blossoms. "That's a very 'elpful sort," it said. "Some may call it *thymus coccineus splendens,* but *I* calls it splendid thyme. An' that ought to be good enough for anybody."

Roger looked at the blossoms. "They're sort of red," he said. "Maybe we'll get the Great Fire of London."

"Or the Russian Revolution!" said Eliza, her eyes kindling.

"Or a volcano," said Ann, timorously.

"Don't worry. It ought to turn out splendidly, from the name," Roger reassured her.

So without further ado, Ann crushed the blossoms in her hand, and each of the children took a spicy whiff. There was a pause.

"It's just like last time," said Ann, wonderingly.

They were still in the garden by the sundial. Not a thing seemed to have happened, except that the sun had crossed the sky and was rapidly sinking in the west, just as it had before.

"Well, of all the cheating things!" said Eliza. "It's just going to be that old Paul Revere thing all over again! The red stands for the Redcoats, I suppose."

"I don't think so," said Roger. "It doesn't feel quite the same, somehow."

"The house isn't the same," said Ann. "It's got trimmings."

Sure enough, the house now had a front porch all covered with gingerbready fretwork that hadn't been there in modern times, nor in Revolutionary War days, either.

And when, a second later, a woman appeared silhouetted against the house, with a lantern in her hand, the shape of her skirts was different, and her voice was different, and the names that she called were different, too.

"John! Abigail! Samantha!" she cried. "Come into the house immediately, out of the night air!"

"I get to take the Natterjack this time," said Eliza, scooping it up quickly. Ann thought that it looked alarmed at the prospect.

"Don't squeeze," it said.

Eliza dropped it in her pocket, and the three children ran to the house.

The mother this time was a stern one, with seemingly unprogressive ideas about child welfare. Either that, or she had something on her mind.

"Children, go to bed at once. It's late," she said, in contradiction of all facts. There was a worried expression in her eyes, and she hardly looked at them as they filed into the long hall.

"You'd think she wanted to get us out of the way!" hissed Eliza to Ann, as they went up the front staircase. There seemed nothing to do but obey, particularly as the woman followed them upstairs and came into the girls' room (the same one they had shared in modern time) and watched to see that they got undressed and put on the old-fashioned nightgowns that were lying in readiness. Then she gave them each a quick kiss and went away, taking the only oil lamp with her, but leaving a single candle to burn in the hall.

As soon as she was out of sight and earshot, Roger stole in from his room, bringing the candle with him, and sat on the foot of Ann's bed.

"What do you suppose is going to happen next?" said Ann, when they'd finished laughing at Roger's red flannel nightshirt. "And when do you suppose it is?"

"Kind of Civil War days, *I'd* say," said Roger, "going by the clothes and the oil lamps."

"Only we're too far north. We'll miss all the fighting," lamented Eliza. "I know one thing, though. I didn't come back through untold decades just to be sent to bed without any supper!"

"You're not hungry yet, are you?" said Roger. "It's only three o'clock in the afternoon by real time."

"*We* know that, but my stomach doesn't," said Eliza. "Dinnertime is dinnertime to it!"

And strangely enough, now that Eliza mentioned it, Ann and Roger found that theirs felt exactly the same way.

"Let's raid the icebox," said Ann.

"Only there wouldn't be any, would there, back in these times? It'd be a larder, more," said Roger.

Ann thought it would be safer to take the Natterjack along, but when Eliza went to look in the pocket of her dress, where she'd hung it up, the Natterjack seemed to be asleep and they hated to disturb it.

Luckily time had wrought no changes inside the house, and they were able to find their way to the kitchen easily, by back passages and stairways, Roger carrying the candle. And luckily the kitchen, when they got there, was deserted. And luckily there was a row of small apple turnovers set out in the larder, to cool.

"Where do you suppose that mother is?" said Ann, between bites.

"I'll reconnoiter," said Eliza. And before the others could stop her, she went tiptoeing toward the front of the house. A few seconds later she was back. "She's watching out the front window," she said. "You mark my words, strange things are afoot in this house tonight!"

After that nobody said anything for a while. There was a sound of munching.

Suddenly Eliza froze, the last bite of crust halfway to her lips. "Hist!" she said.

The others had heard it, too — a stealthy knocking at the front door. Then came quick footsteps, and the sound of bolts being shot back and locks creaking. There was a whisper of voices in the front hall, then more footsteps, those of several people this time, and coming nearer.

The three children had just time to dart behind the door before a strange procession entered the kitchen.

The mother came first, followed by a man in traveling clothes, followed by three others. And at sight of those three forms, Ann and Roger and Eliza knew in a moment what the secret of the house was, and why the mother had been so anxious to get them to bed and out of the way. The time must be just *before* the Civil War, and the house was a station on the Underground Railroad, and the three forms were runaway slaves being helped to escape from the South.

"Only it's out of their way, isn't it, if they're trying to get to Canada?" whispered Ann.

"Shush. Maybe they had to detour," said Roger.

One of the runaway slaves was a boy no older than Roger; the other two seemed to be his father and mother. The boy's eyes gleamed with excitement and he wiped his shining forehead with a red bandanna handkerchief.

And now the mother of John and Abigail and Samantha was saying something about the travelers' being hungry after their journey, and Ann was just wondering what would happen when she found three turnovers missing, when there was an interruption.

A loud clatter of hoofs sounded from without, followed by a banging at the front door. The faces of the runaways turned gray with fright. The boy jumped, and dropped his bandanna.

"Quick!" cried the mother of John and Abigail and Samantha. "Out through the summer kitchen and across the well yard into the barn."

"I had best show them the way," said the man in traveling clothes. And he and the runaway slaves hurried out a farther door. The mother waited till they were safely gone, then went to answer the knocking.

"Look!" muttered Eliza hoarsely, in *their* hiding place. "That boy dropped his red handkerchief! It's incriminating evidence!"

"Don't worry, I'll suppress it," said Roger. But before he could venture forth, more people came into the kitchen.

There was a splendidly dressed man and a queenly woman and a little girl in lace pantalettes, with long golden curls and a spoiled expression. They stood looking around the kitchen as though disdaining it utterly. They did not see the red bandanna, as yet. Their noses were too high in the air.

The mother of John and Abigail and Samantha followed them in, conversing indignantly with another man.

"What is the meaning of this intrusion, Sheriff Watkins?" she was saying.

"Beg pardon, ma'am," said the sheriff. "Must uphold the law, you know, whether we believe in it or not. Three runaway slaves be hiding somewheres in this here neighborhood!"

"Nonsense," said the mother. "Why should runaway slaves proceed to Canada by way of the South Shore?"

"It so happens," interposed the splendidly dressed gentleman, in lofty tones, "that I was called to Boston, for business reasons. My family accompanied me, to observe the customs of the North."

"And we don't think much of them," shrilled the golden-haired little girl, unexpectedly. "Do we, Mamma?"

"Hush, Lily Sue," said the lady fondly, toying with her offspring's ringlets. Eliza, behind the door, exhibited symptoms of nausea.

"We of course brought with us," continued the lofty gentleman, "our personal slaves. My valet, my wife's maid, and our daughter's boy. But whilst we were attending a performance of *Uncle Tom's Cabin* (a drama which I believe should be stopped by law and its author jailed), your base abolitionists have stolen our property! They were followed to this place."

"There be fresh tracks of horses in the yard," added the sheriff, noncommittally.

"To be sure," said the mother of John and Abigail and Samantha. "My brother has just returned from Boston."

"Riding several horses at once?" sneered the lofty gentleman.

"Bringing several newly purchased mounts with him," continued the mother, with apparently unruffled calm. "He is in the barn, seeing to their stabling now."

At that moment the man in traveling clothes returned, by the farther door. "What is amiss, Amelia?" he said.

A babble of explanation and contradictions followed. In the midst of it another rather loutish looking man appeared. He seemed to be the sheriff's helper, but he seemed more interested in toadying up to the lofty gentleman.

"I been searching the upstairs premises," he said. "There be three beds turned down but not slept in!"

"My children's beds," said the mother. "But they should be in them asleep at this hour! Where can they be?" And for the first time she looked alarmed.

"A likely story," said the lofty gentleman, his eyes traveling to the open larder where the forgotten candle now guttered. "And what of those pastries yonder? Why are there three missing from the line?"

"Crumbs on the floor, Beauregard!" cried his wife, looking down and around her with eagle eyes. "Short piecrust, to judge by the flakiness!"

"And there's Bono's handkerchief," put in the unpleasant Lily Sue, seeing the red bandanna at last and picking it up. "I'd know it anywhere!"

This was too much for Eliza. "Oh, you would,

would you?" she cried, abandoning all concealment and springing forth into the midst of the group. Ann and Roger were only a second behind her. "It so happens that handkerchief is *mine*," went on the intrepid girl. "I *always* use red handkerchiefs. Give it to me." And she laid hold of the bandanna.

"Manners, Abigail," cried the mother, but Ann thought that she sounded admiring.

A short tug of war followed. Eliza won easily. The child Lily Sue began to cry.

"*We* ate the pies, Mamma," said Ann, remembering that she was supposed to be the mother's daughter Samantha.

"We were hungry and couldn't sleep," said Roger.

"You see?" said the mother to the others, rather proudly, Ann thought.

"I don't believe it," said the lofty gentleman. "Why should abolitionist children tell the truth any more than their parents?"

"They have nasty lying faces, Beauregard," said the queenly lady, "and they made Lily Sue cry!"

At this the wretched Lily Sue began to cry louder.

"I'm afraid, ma'am," said the sheriff, regretfully, "I'll have to search the outbuildings."

But at this moment help came from an unexpected quarter.

The Natterjack had apparently wakened, found itself alone, and wished for company. Now Roger, looking through the open door into the front hall-way, watched in fascination as it appeared, hopping nonchalantly down the staircase. At the bottom it turned, and started along the passage. From the kitchen door it took an immense leap and landed full in the face of the queenly lady. The queenly lady uttered a shriek.

"Ugh! The horrid thing! Take it away!" she cried, beating at the air about her head.

The Natterjack regarded her coldly from a perch on her shoulder. She met its gaze, moaned, and sank half swooning into a chair.

"Remove that beast!" commanded the lofty gentleman, taking no steps to remove it himself, and eyeing it with distaste.

"It's only our pet toad," said Ann, hoping the Natterjack would forgive her for this insulting description.

"Yes," said Roger, getting a sudden idea. "We forgot to feed it and it came down for its supper."

"Take it out of the room, take it out of the room!" cried the lady, in a faint voice.

"I was just going to," said Roger, picking the Natterjack up gently. "Bring the pies, Ann. I mean Samantha."

Seeing the point at once, Ann took three more turnovers from the larder shelf.

"Strange-like fare that be for an old toad," said the hateful helper of the sheriff, eyeing them suspiciously.

"The best piecrust," Eliza told him haughtily, "is none too good for any pet of ours!" And bearing the Natterjack (and the turnovers), the three children marched out of the house.

Once outside, however, their calm gave way. Everyone talked at once, but Eliza was loudest. "What'll we do?" she cried. "We've got to get them fed and rescued, and that sheriff'll be out searching the barn in no time at all!"

The Natterjack seemed to have grasped the situation without having it explained. "You take your thyme," it said. "Rub an' whiff, and wish you'd been there five minutes ago."

"Can we do that?" said Ann. "Will it work?"

"I told you before," said the Natterjack, "that's

splendid thyme you've got there. So long as your h'aims are splendid, it'll accommodate itself." And it gave the three children a nod of unusual approval.

So Ann (who luckily had remembered to tuck the sprig of thyme in her nightgown sleeve when she got undressed) rubbed, and they all whiffed, and the next moment they and the Natterjack were standing in the great gloomy barn.

At first it seemed to be deserted. Then by the light of the moon outside the window the three children saw three pairs of eyes looking down at them cautiously from the hayloft.

"Here. Quick," said Roger, and he and Ann held out the apple turnovers. "We're sorry to start with dessert," he went on, as the hungry travelers jumped down from the loft and fell to eating, "but you'll be where you can get more soon."

"I'll make it be dinnertime when they get to Canada," said Ann. "I'll make it be a time when they served free dinner to all runaway slaves." She looked at the Natterjack to see if this were the way to get wishes by thyme-travel. Again the Natterjack gave an approving nod.

"Wait," said Eliza. "There's something I have to do here, first." So the others waited.

What Eliza did was climb up to the loft and prop a whole stack of moldy hay against the half-open barn door, where it would plop down on the heads of any who tried to enter.

"There," she said, jumping down from the loft. "*That's* taken care of."

And she was none too soon, for a sound of running feet was heard from without, showing that the extra five minutes were up. Quickly Ann rubbed her sprig of thyme. The three children took a deep whiff, and Ann wished.

It was thoughtful of the magic to pick Niagara Falls as the place for them to enter Canada, for none of the three children had ever been there before, and the sight was thrilling. Eliza for one could hardly be torn away from the water's edge, and wanted to go over the falls in a barrel right now. And when the others dissuaded her, she wanted to sit down and have some of the dinner the runaway slaves were enjoying. For Ann had wished it to be dinnertime when they arrived, and so of course it *was,* and the three children were hungry all over again.

But Ann thought they had best be getting back to the house by the sea, for fear the mother of John and Abigail and Samantha would be worrying.

When the three children said good-bye to the three runaways, the ex-slaves fell on their knees and kissed their hands in gratitude.

"Don't do that," Roger told them. "Don't ever kneel to anybody or kiss anybody's hand again. You're free people now."

"Hallelujah! Praise the Lord!" said the ex-slaves.

At the last moment Eliza remembered the red bandanna and tried to give it back to the boy Bono, but he begged her to keep it as a gift, in token of everlasting gratitude, and Eliza was nothing loath.

And again Ann rubbed her sprig of thyme (which instead of getting worn out by all the rubbing seemed to be growing perkier and more bloomy with each splendid wish), and the next moment she and Roger and Eliza found themselves back in the kitchen.

An unpleasant scene was in progress. The success of Eliza's booby trap had been all that she could have hoped for. The sheriff and his helper and the lofty gentleman had burst in the barn door, and the lofty gentleman had been in the lead and had borne the brunt of it.

His top hat was crushed and there were wisps of hay sticking in his side whiskers and tickling him inside his collar and cluttering his fine suit. He was shaking his fist now and hurling threats at everyone in sight.

"Just let me get my hands on those three young scamps!" he was saying. "They planned this, *besides* stealing my slaves!"

"Not at all," said the mother. "We *always* leave the barn door arranged so. It's a special invention for keeping out unwelcome intruders. My little girl invented it. She's very clever." And her eyes smiled at Eliza.

The lofty gentleman whirled on the three children. "So *there* you are!" he said. "What have you done with my stolen property?"

"We haven't done anything with *anybody's* property," said Roger. And he was telling the truth, for how can one man be the property of another?

"'Pears like he's right," muttered the sheriff, scratching his head (which also contained its portion of hay). "Horses was all stabled. Warn't no time to get away on foot. Warn't no place to hide, neither!"

The gentleman opened his mouth to retort. Then he couldn't think of anything to say. He shut it again, and turned to his wife. "Come, Veronica!" he said.

"I have seen enough of Yankee customs! We're going back to Virginia this very minute!" And jamming his ruined hat on his head, he stalked out the door. His wife sailed after him, her nose in the air. The child Lily Sue followed, beginning to cry again.

"Oh, stop that sniveling!" the voice of Lily Sue's mother was heard in the hall, followed by a loud slap, and then silence.

Back in the kitchen everyone giggled with relief, even the sheriff. A moment later he and his helper took their leave, with many apologies.

As soon as they were safely gone, the mother ran to embrace the three children. "John! Abigail! Samantha! What happened? Where did you put our three friends?"

"We got them away. They're going to be free now," said Roger, feeling this was as close to the truth as he could come without awkward questions.

"And to think," cried the mother in self-reproach, "that I tried to keep it from you! I thought you were too young to know. But you have proved otherwise. From now on, you may help me with the Underground Railroad as long as the need for it continues. But now back to bed. Even heroes must have their sleep. Put that nasty toad out in the garden first. I can't think how it can have got in the house."

"Can't we take it to bed with us just this once?" pleaded Ann, fearful that the Natterjack might be mislaid and left behind in the nineteenth century (though she need not have worried. All time is the same to a Natterjack).

"Oh very well, this once," said the mother. "Why you should choose such a horrid pet I cannot imagine. Though after all it *was* helpful tonight," she added, with a relenting smile.

The three children went upstairs, Eliza carrying the Natterjack. They put on their own clothes and assembled in the girls' room. Ann rubbed her sprig of thyme.

"There," she said a moment later, poking the sprig back into the flowery bank, where it attached itself and grew again.

"And a splendid time was had by all," sighed Eliza, in tones of satisfaction.

The three children lolled back on the blossomy slope under the sun of a twentieth-century midafternoon. The Natterjack squatted nearby, digesting a leafhopper.

"What I'm wondering," said Eliza, after a bit, "is about the real John and Abigail and Samantha. Where were they while we were there? And did all that happen to them, too, or just to us?"

"Anyway," said Roger almost enviously, "they're going to have a wonderful time from now on, helping runaway slaves practically every night."

"So that's another good turn we did, *besides* helping Bono get to Canada," said Ann.

"One good turn deserves another," said Eliza, "and we did two. We ought to get a specially good adventure next time."

"No bargaining," muttered the Natterjack. "Wait till your next chance comes."

"When'll *that* be?" said Eliza.

"All in good time," said the Natterjack. And it hopped away, leaving them with that to puzzle over.

Later that day Eliza remembered the red bandanna handkerchief and realized she'd left it in her nightgown pocket when she changed clothes, back in eighteen fifty-something. "Darn," she said. "I wanted it for a souvenir." Then Ann called her for a game of hide-and-seek and she forgot all about it.

It was two days afterward, on a morning of rain and northeast wind, that old Mrs. Whiton suggested Ann and Eliza and Roger might enjoy playing in the attic. And they did, for the attic was full of wonderful things like old chess sets and models of clipper ships and bound volumes of *The St. Nicholas Magazine*.

It was Ann who wondered what was in the big cedar chest in the corner and it was Roger who figured out how to open it. But it was Eliza who found the red bandanna handkerchief, neatly folded on top of the things inside (which otherwise proved to be dull old extra sheets).

"It's the same one! I know it is!" she cried. "It's got the place where it tore a little when we tug-of-warred it!"

"Let's ask old Mrs. Whiton," said Ann, and they ran to find her.

"So *that's* where it's been," said old Mrs. Whiton, straightening out the bandanna's faded folds. "I haven't seen it in years. Bono's kerchief, we always called it. It was given to my husband's great-aunt Abigail by a runaway slave boy she saved on the Underground Railroad."

"So you see?" said Eliza, when the three children

were alone again. "The real John and Abigail and Samantha *must* have been there all along!"

"Then are they us?" said Roger ungrammatically, trying to puzzle it out, "or are we them?"

"Don't," said Ann. "That kind of thing makes my head ache. It's worse than long division."

"I guess it's all just part of the Mystery of Time," said Roger, sagely.

"And we've only just begun to explore it," said Eliza. "Compared with what's still to come, we haven't seen *anything* yet, hardly!"

And they hadn't.

4

All in Good Time

"I'm disappointed," said Eliza.

"What in?" said Roger, shouting to be heard over the waves, for the three children were sitting on the beach at high tide, several mornings later.

"The magic," said Eliza.

"I don't see how you can say that," said Ann. "It's been just lovely."

"Oh, it's been all right in its way," said Eliza, "so far. Only it's all been kind of nonfiction! Like those books where you get Highlights of History, with kind of a story wrapped around. Or those television shows where You are There. We've had the Revolution and the Civil War. Any day now we'll get around to the election of Calvin Coolidge. There's no variety."

"Variety is the surprise of life," said Ann, who had heard this somewhere.

"Exactly," said Eliza. "Without it all is dead bones."

"We've learned how to use the thyme wishes better," Roger pointed out. "Once we get started we can just keep on wishing it were time for whatever it is we want to wish for next!"

"It'll be simple from now on," said Ann. "All we do is, we look in the garden catalog first and pick out a kind of thyme that sounds like fun."

"Are we to be the mere toys and baubles of mere plant life?" said Eliza. "Suppose the time I want to go to isn't in their old catalog?"

"We could hybridize," suggested Roger, dubiously.

"You mean go to sleep for the winter?" said Ann.

"No," said Roger. "It means crossing two kinds of plants. I think you kind of mix the pollen."

"And then wait around for a year to see what happens!" scoffs Eliza. "*That's* no good!"

"Anyway, there're enough kinds already," said

Ann. "There's golden thyme that we haven't tried, and lemon thyme and . . ."

"Oh, sure," said Eliza, "and learn all about fruit-growing in sunny California! That'll be dandy!"

"You're just out of sorts," said Roger. "You must have got out of the wrong side of the bed this morning. Let's throw her in the ocean and wake her up."

So they did, and all argument dissolved in the briny joy of sheer wateriness. But their swim was of short duration.

Old Mrs. Whiton appeared and called from the rock stair. "Children, come in." So they went in, and climbed the steps to find her still waiting at the top. "Hurry and dress," she said. "Today we're going to Boston." And since old Mrs. Whiton's word was law in that house, they hurried to do just that.

Strange as it might seem, it turned out Jack had no engagement with a teenage girl that day. "I might as well come along, too," he said, which was most unusual of him.

As the girls were dressing in their room, Ann had a sudden thought. "Jack's coming," she said.

"I know," said Eliza.

"Well," said Ann, "I was sort of thinking. He almost never does. We almost never have a good time together, all of us. And I was thinking. 'All in good time,' the Natterjack said. This must be it!"

"First one dressed gets to ask," said Eliza.

The race was very nearly a tie. Eliza rushed down the stairs and out into the garden only a few seconds ahead of Ann. Roger appeared, saw where they were going, and followed.

The Natterjack lay upon the sundial, awake but torpid. It didn't seem interested in going anywhere or doing anything, even when Ann explained about the trip to Boston, and Jack's coming along.

Ann's face fell. "Oh," she said, disappointed. "I thought . . ."

"You said 'All in good time,' " Eliza reminded the Natterjack, accusingly.

"Did I say that?" said the Natterjack.

"Yes," said Eliza, "you did."

"Well . . ." It seemed to hesitate. "It would be 'ighly irregular. I 'aven't been off this 'ere acre in 'alf a century. Besides, where would I find the thyme?"

"We could take a supply along," suggested Roger.

"No being carried in pockets, mind," said the Natterjack. " 'Orrid close they is, for breathing."

"Don't worry, you'll have every comfort," Eliza assured it.

She and Roger and Ann raced for the kitchen. To wheedle an empty coffee tin from Mrs. Annable was the work of but a moment.

Back in the garden, Ann and Eliza made a soothing nest of thyme clippings for the Natterjack to repose on, in the bottom of the coffee tin. They put in snippets of as many different kinds of the creeping plant as they could find, just in case. Eliza put in any random creeping insects she came upon, too, for fear the Natterjack might feel hungry en route. Roger made air holes in the top of the tin with the can-opener blade of his jackknife. Ann lifted the Natterjack carefully from the sundial and placed it tenderly on its flowery cushion. It relaxed, and almost seemed to smile. Roger fixed the lid on tight.

"There!" said Eliza. "The three faithful attendants bore the Sleeping Beauty to the waiting chariot!" For the Willys-Knight was already honking in the driveway. Eliza and Roger and Ann ran toward it, Roger carrying the Natterjack-tin carefully in a horizontal position.

If old Mrs. Whiton noticed the tin, she did not mention it. She had decided to drive into Boston herself today, which she did sitting straight and fierce, and flinging her arm out so wide and wildly at the turns that Ann was afraid she might dislocate something. She spoke little except to point out an occasional point of interest, but Jack was in an unusually good mood, regaling the company with song and story as they drove, till it seemed no time at all before the tall buildings of Boston began to show in the distance, and all was billboards and filling stations.

"It's like having the old Jack back with us again," muttered Eliza to Ann. "All he needs now is a magic adventure to make him practically as good as new." And she cast a meaningful glance in the direction of the tinned Natterjack.

If you have ever been to Boston (and everyone should go there at least once), you will know that as a city it is a bewildering mixture of modern improvements and the relics of antiquity, and it is interesting, for example, to come out from buying plastic clothes-pins and chocolate-strawberry-marshmallow-banana splits in a department store glittering with neon, and find yourself face to face with the Old South Church. And the streets have wonderful old names like Milk and Pump.

Jack had brought his color camera along, and took snapshots of all the important landmarks, and more than once Ann's eyes or Roger's wandered hopefully toward the Natterjack, when they came to a historic spot that might make a thrilling adventure. When old Mrs. Whiton drove them past the Bunker Hill monument, Roger wanted to plunge back through time and enlist in the battle right now, and when they went by the harbor where the Boston Tea Party had been, even the shy and retiring Ann yearned to be there with blackened face, tomahawking tea casks right and left with the rest of the Sons of Liberty.

But Eliza was adamant. "No," she said. "It would be instructive—in disguise—and that's one thing I won't bear!"

After the harbor, old Mrs. Whiton said there was one more surprise she'd like to show them, if they didn't mind going home a long way round, and of course they didn't. So then they drove over a bridge like pepper pots, and along the still waters of the Charles River, and past the red-and-white buildings of Harvard University (only that wasn't the surprise), and after that the scenery started getting more country-ish again. Pretty soon they passed a sign that read, "Concord, five miles." Eliza nudged the others.

"More history," she muttered. "Those old minutemen again. We've *had* that!"

But when they came into the town itself, her heart

relented, and she and Jack and Ann and Roger didn't need to know anything about New England architecture to realize that Concord was a perfect place, with its beautiful, serene old gabled houses looking as if they had been sitting there squarely and at peace forever.

Old Mrs. Whiton drove slowly past one of the oldest-looking houses, a small brown one, and brought the car to a stop. "This," she said, "is the house where Louisa Alcott lived. It's the house she wrote about in *Little Women*. I thought you might like to get out and take a really good look."

Her last words were unnecessary. Eliza and Ann were already clambering out of the backseat, with rapt faces.

"Aren't you coming?" said Roger to Jack.

"Who cares?" Jack yawned. "It's just an old girls' book." But he got out of the car.

"I don't think it's just for girls, exactly," said Roger. "I think it's sort of for everybody, more."

The four children stood looking at the house.

"It looks just the way I thought it would, always," breathed Ann, in reverent tones. "You can just *see* Meg and Jo and Beth and Amy living in it!"

A glint appeared in the eyes of Eliza. "Why not?" she said.

Ann looked at her, a wild surmise in her face. Her heart thumped. "Could we?"

It was but the work of a second for Eliza to run to the car and fetch the coffee tin with the Natterjack.

"This is crazy," said Jack. "Even if there were anything to the magic, you couldn't go back in time to *them!* They weren't real. They didn't ever happen."

"They did, too," said Ann. "She wrote about herself and her sisters, just the way it was!"

"It's real-er than anything in your old history books!" cried Eliza. "Anyway, we went back in time to Ivanhoe, didn't we, last summer?" She was struggling with the lid of the coffee tin. It came off, and the Natterjack awoke and looked out. It seemed to recognize its surroundings right away.

"So *this* is what you picked," it said. "You might 'ave done worse."

"Excuse me," said Ann, reaching under it for one of the thyme snippets. The piece that her fingers fell on turned out to be a sprig of the golden kind.

"That's very appropriate," said Roger, learnedly. "It was the golden age of New England, just about."

Ann rubbed the bit of thyme, and even Jack sheepishly joined the others as they leaned over to catch a sniff of its fragrance. Then they stood looking around them.

Everything was the same and yet everything was different. Old Mrs. Whiton and the car were nowhere to be seen. It was winter. And it was snowing. (For who can think of the March family without thinking of snowballs and mittens and skating on the pond and Christmas coming any minute?)

"Gee," said Jack. "There must be something to it, after all. I'm just in my sports shirt and cotton pants and I don't feel a bit cold."

"That's the way with thyme-magic," said Roger. "Probably we're all in alpaca coats and beaver hats, as *they* see us." He gestured at two figures that were approaching along the walk.

The snowflakes were falling so thickly that it was hard to see who the figures were. But at this moment the foremost one spoke, and after that nobody needed to be told.

"Christopher Columbus!" said the figure. And Miss Josephine March, Jo herself, came running toward them with her lanky stride, and then stood regarding them in a gentlemanly manner, with her hands behind her back, her feet well apart and her thick chestnut hair escaping from under her cap, just as it always did. Ann and Eliza could only stare back, too moved for speech.

"Do not *prance,* Jo! Don't stand with your hands behind your back, and try not to use such tomboy-ish slang," said the second figure, following more sedately and proving to be a pretty girl with brown hair and pink cheeks who could only be the sensible, ladylike Meg.

Ann found her tongue at last. "Hello," she said. "You're Jo and Meg. I'm Ann. These are Roger and Jack and Eliza. Where are the others?"

"Beth has a slight cold," said Meg, "and Amy is spending the week with Aunt March."

Ann and Roger and Eliza felt relieved, on the whole. Because in the book Beth dies, and there isn't much you can do about people who die in books except hope their days were happy though numbered, and that it was worth it. As for Amy, neither Ann and Roger and Eliza nor anyone else has ever yet forgiven her for marrying Laurie in the end, when anyone could *tell* he was meant for Jo!

Jo was peppering them with questions now, and not waiting for the answers. "Are you a new family just moved to Concord? We *will* have times! Have you met Laurie, the boy next door? You're sure to like him, for he's a capital fellow!"

"Oh, I *know!*" said Ann and Eliza, adoringly.

"Come on!" said Jo, striding toward the big stone house nearby. Ann and Roger and Eliza followed. Then they looked back. Jack wasn't coming on. He was staring at Meg, and his face was red and his eyes were taking on a glazed expression. His behavior, in short, was all too familiar.

"Good grief!" said Eliza. "That's one thing I never thought of. That Meg. You know what she is? She's a *teenage girl!*"

"It's good-bye to hope," Ann agreed. "He might just as well not be here from this moment on!"

Jo looked where they were looking, and glowered. "Let's not take any notice," she said. "I hate sentimental nonsense, spoiling all the fun." And she strode on with her shoulders hunched and her hands in her jacket pockets.

Laurie must have seen them from his window, for now there was a cry of "What ho?" and he came running down the steps of his house to meet them, looking just as everybody had known he would look, with his bright black eyes and his curly black hair.

Roger liked him right away, and as for the girls, they had been his willing slaves since long ago.

"What shall it be this afternoon?" he said, after everyone had been introduced. "A grand dramatic entertainment called 'The Witch's Curse,' or sledding, with apples and gingerbread to follow?"

A short whispered colloquy ensued.

"Shall we tell them?" said Roger.

"Why not?" said Eliza. "Those two would be fine to have along on *any* adventure!"

"Let's not," said Ann. "Let's stay here and have sledding and apples and gingerbread. I *like* Concord."

But she was overruled. A second later Roger and Eliza were telling all about the thyme-magic and introducing the Natterjack, in its coffee tin. Jo and Laurie were impressed.

"Tell me about the twentieth century," said Jo. "Is the Civil War over and the slaves freed and everything perfect?"

"Well, maybe not quite," said Roger, "but we're getting better all the time."

Laurie, ever less serious, brushed this aside. "Let's talk about *now,*" he said. "Magic adventures are the one thing that's been needed to make this the best year ever! How do we begin? Do we make wishes?"

"There are a hundred things I could wish for," sighed Jo. "The butcher's bill paid and a new parlor carpet. If I could begin selling the stories I write, I could help. Could I wish it were time for that?"

Ann thought this would be nice, but perhaps not exciting enough for Eliza. "Anyway, all that comes later," she said. "You sell lots and lots of stories."

"I do?" said Jo.

"Yes," said Ann. "Only you stop writing wild romances and just tell about your life here, in this house."

"*That* wouldn't make a story," said Jo.

"It does, though," said Roger, not exactly sure at this moment whether he were addressing his remarks to Miss Josephine March or to Louisa May Alcott herself, but it didn't matter because they were the same person, really. "It makes a story that'll never be forgotten as long as there are children anywhere."

"Christopher Columbus!" said Jo, staring into the future with wide eyes.

"Now then, that's enough, Miss Charlotte Brontë George Eliot March!" said Laurie, his eyes twinkling. "Come down to earth and shed your genius on *us!* Tell us what we're going to do *today!* Forget duty for once, and let's be thoroughly selfish and frivolous!"

"For goodness' sake *let's!*" said Eliza, jigging from one foot to the other. "Less talk, more action!"

"Very well!" said Jo, casting sober thoughts sky-high with a grin. "We'll fly round and have larks! We'll go to the Orkney Islands! Or off with the wraggle-taggle Gypsies, O! Or over the hills and far away!"

"Let's make it Gypsies," said Eliza. "I'll be the beautiful Gypsy fortuneteller. A king's son will cross my palm with silver and fall in love with me! I'll . . ."

But there was an interruption. A tall motherly-looking woman had appeared in the doorway of the house. Jo ran to her. Meg detached herself from the conversation of Jack and joined them.

"Oh my girls," said the woman, "in our happiness we must not forget others less fortunate than ourselves. I have just heard some sad news."

"Wouldn't you know?" muttered Eliza to Ann. "She always did!"

"Not a mile from here," continued Mrs. March, for of course it was she, "lies a poor sick woman with a young baby and neither food nor firewood, and no money to purchase either! I leave it to my dear girls to think what best to do for her."

"I'll cut logs, Marmee!" cried Jo. "I'm as good a

hand with an ax and saw as any boy in Concord."

"There is a pound of scrag of mutton in the larder," said Meg. "I was planning to try a French ragout such as the Moffats always serve, but it will make a nourishing stew for the poor woman, and we can dine on tea and toast."

Mrs. March rewarded her daughters with a proud smile and a quiet "Well done."

"Oh, for goodness' sake!" said Eliza, indignantly. "It's as bad as the time they had to give up their breakfast on Christmas morning and have bread and milk instead! We can't do good deeds now; we're just starting an important adventure!"

Mrs. March said nothing, merely folding her lips tightly and giving Eliza a long look. So of course after that Eliza had to be noble and self-sacrificing, too.

"At least we can go by thyme-travel and not walk a mile, can't we?" she said, after Mrs. March had gone inside. "We'll get there earlier and have that much more time for nobleness!"

And all agreed that this was only logical.

Meg fetched the scrag of mutton from the larder and Jack offered to carry it for her and seemed not to mind the greasiness of the paper. Jo and Laurie ran for the ax and saw. Ann rubbed the sprig of golden thyme.

The next moment they and the Natterjack found themselves in a dusty and disorderly one-room hovel. A woman, looking more lazy than ill, lolled on a rumpled bed reading a book called *How He Won Her,* while the baby, a lusty boy of three, sat in a corner, knocking a battered doll against the wall.

"Who are you?" said the woman.

"We've come to help," said Meg.

"How nice," said the woman. "I always say the Lord will provide!" And she lay back on her pillows and watched complacently as Jo and Laurie ran for the wood lot, Roger found sticks for kindling and laid a fire on the ill-kept hearth, and Meg dealt with the scrag of mutton while Jack watched in mute admiration.

The dry sink in the corner was crowded with dirty dishes. "Am I supposed to tackle these?" grumbled Eliza. "I didn't come back through the mists of time to do *menial labors!*"

"Maybe the magic's teaching you a lesson," said Roger, from the hearth. "It did once before."

"The nerve!" said Eliza. But she fell to nevertheless, pumping water from the well, fetching it pail by pail, and working so hard that by the time Laurie and Jo came stamping in laughing and rosy-cheeked with armfuls of logs, the dishes were in apple-pie order, and Jo pronounced Eliza "a trump" and "a brick."

Ann meanwhile had decided to amuse the baby. But do what she would, the baby didn't seem to appreciate her efforts. When she tried playing pat-a-cake with it, it threw its doll at her. And when she began telling it a story, it hit her in the eye with an old chewed building block. Then it noticed her birthstone ring with the real garnet.

"Pretty. Baby want," it said. And pulling the ring from Ann's finger it clutched it tightly in its own hot hand.

"Naughty. Mustn't do," said Ann. "Give ringy back to Ann."

"Won't," said the baby, pouting. "Nassy dirl." And it turned and ran to its mother.

"What are you doing to my child?" demanded the woman, looking up from her book. Then her tone changed as she saw the ring. "Why, how nice!" she cried, taking it and slipping it on her own finger.

"And red is my favorite color, too! Baby, say thank you to the young lady for giving it to Mama!"

"But I didn't!" gasped Ann. "It's my present from birthday before last!"

The woman looked hurt. "How can you talk so?" she whined. "And you with so much and us with so little! Never did I think one of you nice young ladies would turn out to be a Indian giver!"

"I'm not! It's all a mistake!" said poor Ann, hating to hurt the woman's feelings, yet not quite trusting her, somehow. She looked round for advice, but the others were busy getting supper. Then she thought of the Natterjack, and took the lid off the coffee tin. But before she could seek its aid, a man appeared in the doorway. He was a big burly fellow with a shifty eye, and Ann didn't like the look of him.

"Supper ready, Eupheemy?" he said, sniffing the air, through which a savory scent was beginning to steal.

"Yes, Clarence, it is, thanks to these ministering angels as ever was," said the woman. "This young lady gave me this ring. Ain't it purty?"

The man inspected the ring. "Semiprecious!" he said, in tones of contempt. He sniffed the air again.

"Mutton stew! Not much class to the bill of fare. They might at least have brought a beefsteak! Don't look like rich young ladies at all. Poorly dressed," he added, looking at Jo's shabby poplin with the burn and the tear.

The others were listening now, and Eliza had heard enough. "Oh, is that so?" she cried, springing forward. "Well, I think you're lucky we bother helping you at all! We may not be rich, but we're more important than you think we are!"

"Oh?" said the man, interested. "Tell me more."

"Well," said Eliza, forgetting all her mother had ever told her about not boasting. "Take Laurie. His grandfather's a prominent citizen."

"You don't say!" said the man, pleased. "Rich old gentleman, I presoom? Nice big house? Stately mansion?"

"Stone," said Eliza, "with pillars."

"Fine. Fine," said the man. "Go on."

"And Jo may be poor," went on the headstrong girl, though Roger was glaring at her and making signs of caution, "but she's going to be a famous author any day now!"

"Well, well," said the man, rubbing his hands together. "'Pears we've got distinguished guests,

Eupheemy! It'd be a pity if they was to get away, wouldn't it? Lock the door!"

The woman sprang from the bed with surprising agility, turned the key, and put it in her pocket. The seven "ministering angels" turned pale, as the man's purpose became plain.

"Now see what you've done," hissed Roger to Eliza. "You've got us kidnapped!"

"Now, now," said the man. "No need to use ugly words. We just want you to set awhile, that's all. Rich men's sonny-boys and lady-authors ought to have friends who'd pay a pretty penny to have 'em back safe an' sound!" And he laughed unpleasantly.

"Don't worry," said Jack rather shakily to Roger and Laurie. "It's three of us fellows against one of him. Stand close together. Form a hollow square with the girls behind us."

But Eliza needed no defending. "You'd better watch out!" she cried to the man. "I happen to be a pretty important sorceress, myself! From the twentieth century! I've got a magic there in that coffee tin that could smash you to atoms! Isn't that so?" she appealed to the Natterjack.

"H'atoms!" agreed the Natterjack, from the coffee tin.

"I don't like this, Clarence," said the woman uneasily. "They got talking beasts. They come from future parts."

"I don't believe it," said the man. "It's ventriloquists. That ain't no beast. That's a measly old frog."

The Natterjack was affronted. "Very well," it said, puffing itself out angrily. "Deceiving these h'innocent children and these 'eroines of fiction was one thing, but h'insulting *me* is the last straw! Who 'as the thyme?"

Ann held out the golden sprig and the Natterjack looked at it. "'Ighly suitable," it said. "The time I 'ave in mind may not 'ave been pleasant for *some*, but it was a golden age for Natterjacks!"

It rubbed the bit of thyme with its foot and whiffed the fragrance. Maybe because nobody else whiffed, the others remained as they were. But a startling change occurred in the vicinity of the coffee tin. The Natterjack disappeared. In its place was a fabulous beast as tall as the ceiling. Gnashing teeth filled its hideous jaws. It had claws, and talons, and a great uncoiling scaly tail that nearly filled the whole room.

"Dragons!" cried Jo, her eyes gleaming.

"I'll defend you!" cried Laurie, reaching for the poker.

"Don't," cried Ann. "It's our Natterjack! It's friendly!"

"Friendly to *some*," said the Natterjack, "but to those as deserves it I can be *'orrible!*" And it lowered its great horrendous head to glare at the man and woman. The woman cowered, trembling, but the man stood his ground, pale but defiant.

"It isn't a dragon, really," Jack explained to the faltering Meg. "There's no such thing. It's a prehistoric beast. *Tyrannosaurus rex,* I think it's called."

"What's in a name?" remarked the Natterjack airily, blowing puffs of smoke from its nostrils. "Some may call us dragons an' some may call us tyrannosauruses, but we're h'*all* Natterjacks h'under the skin!"

"You've kind of dwindled down, in modern times, haven't you?" said Roger.

"Not at all," said the Natterjack. "What we once put into brawn, we puts into brain. When you think 'ow much h'extra brain that makes left over, h'it's no *wonder* we're magic! H'it *does* feel good to get back into form again once in a while, though." It swished its tail, knocking over several chairs and a table, and breathed out more puffs of brimstone-y smelling smoke. "H'I can't manage smoke rings again yet," it added. "H'out of practice!"

There was a pause. "Well?" said Eliza. "Aren't you going to eat them?"

The Natterjack hesitated. "By rights I should," it said, eyeing the man and woman with distaste, "but I doubt if they'd digest, from the look of them. They'd sit 'eavy. Per'aps if they was to reform, I'd h'overlook it this once."

"Reform, Clarence," begged the woman. "Reform before it's too late!"

"I won't!" said the man stubbornly. "I won't *never*. I'd sooner be et!"

"Oh, very well," sighed the Natterjack. And it opened its jaws.

But there was an interruption. "Wait!" cried Jo. "Two wrongs do not make a right, and violence never yet solved anything in this world."

She advanced on the man and woman. With her face flushed in righteous anger and her hair escaping from its pins and coming down behind, she made a glorious sight. And even in the heat of the moment Ann noticed that Jack had stopped looking at Meg and was staring at Jo with the reddening cheek and glazing eye of utter adoration. And she remembered suddenly that Jo was a teenage girl, too!

"Aren't you ashamed of yourself?" said Jo to the man.

"No I ain't," said the man. "Take or be took by, that's the rule of life. Grab or be downtrod!"

"No such thing," said Jo. "If you would put your shoulder to the wheel and learn to know the happy weariness that comes from honest toil, you would see things differently."

"Wouldn't neither," said the man. "I tried working once. All I got was tired and no richer."

"Think of the terrible influence on your poor family, if you go on as you are," said Jo. "Already they are showing the effects of an unfavorable environment. I don't mean to be rude, but your wife is *not* a good housekeeper. And your baby is undisciplined."

"It certainly is," said Ann. "It stole my ring with the garnet."

"It did?" said the man, pleased. "Clever little fellow!"

Jo was still not discouraged. "You must have a better side *somewhere*," she said. "No matter how hardened in crime you are, you, too, must have been an innocent baby once. You, too, must have had a mother!"

"I never!" said the man. "I was born an orphing."

"You must have had *someone*," insisted Jo.

For the first time the man's hard exterior showed signs of softening. "Aunt Jerusha!" he murmured. "Good old Aunt Jerusha! Hain't thought of her these forty years!"

"Exactly," said Jo, triumphant. "Then think of her now. Think of that gentlewoman caring for you and watching you flower into manhood!"

"She *warn't* gentle!" said the man, indignantly. "She were tough! Cuff you as soon as look at you, she would!" And his face relaxed in a look of happy remembrance. Jo was quick to press home her advantage.

"Think of her poor hands, weary with cuffing!" she said. "Think of her arm, weary with switching. Think of her face, worn with the care of thinking up new punishments, all in hope that you'd grow into a good man! And think of how you have repaid her!"

The man looked from Jo to the Natterjack-dragon and back again. His lip trembled. "'Tain't fair," he said. "Gangin' up on a man's soft spots, reformin' him against his will! 'Tain't no-ways fair!"

"Why don't you give in?" said Ann. "It's easy being good, when you get started."

"It's fun, too, in a way," said Eliza, "now and then."

The man hesitated. Then he made up his mind. "All right," he said. "I've tried everything else. Might as well try *that!*" And his iron control gave way, and he burst into sobs of repentance. "Ain't it awful?" he said, between sobs. "Ain't it horrible to think what I've went an' become? Maybe it's 'cause Aunt Jerusha died and there warn't no more cuffing! Maybe if one of you was to cuff me now, I'd be a better man!"

Laurie and Jack and Roger were perfectly willing, but Jo dissuaded them. "No," she said. "He has reformed at last, and that is punishment enough."

"Yes," said Ann, carried away by the emotion of the moment, "let's turn the other cheek and heap coals of fire on it!"

"Do I have to give the ring back, too, Clarence?" asked the woman.

"Yes, Eupheemy, you do," said the man. "If we're going to reform, might as well go the whole hog!" And the woman handed it over.

Everyone was being so noble that Ann almost

hated to take it. If it hadn't been a present from her favorite Aunt Jane, she wouldn't have.

"Of course," said the Natterjack, speaking for the first time in quite a while, "that isn't *quite* h'all there is to it. H'it isn't quite as h'easy as *that!* There 'as to be signs of h'improvement in future. The *first* thing to do is clean up this messy room!"

And urged on by gentle shoves from the Natterjack's dragonlike claws and hot gusts of its smoky breath, the man and woman proceeded to give the room such a thorough cleaning as it had never known in all its days, dusting and sweeping and scouring and waxing till they were nearly dropping with weariness. When it came time for beating the carpets on the line in the yard, the Natterjack took pity on the man and woman and offered the use of its tail. All the neighbors and passersby took one look at the carpet-beating dragon, and rushed inside and locked the doors and sent for the police, and the man and woman were later forced to move out of town, for harboring undesirable pets. But that is another story.

"And now," said Eliza to the Natterjack, when the house cleaning was finally over, "let's all go back to dragon-time with you. Did you used to eat many princesses? Was it you who fought Saint George? Can we watch?"

"Let's not," said Ann. "Let's go back to Concord and have sledding and apples and gingerbread instead."

The Natterjack shook its head regretfully. "H'I'm afraid we can't do h'either," it said. "When this 'ere magic stops, it stops. The next whiff will take h'each of us back to 'is own century. It's time to say good-bye."

"Couldn't we have a stopover on the way?" pleaded Ann, loath to leave the magnificent Jo behind in time forever. As for Jack, he said nothing, but his face as he looked at Jo was more crimson and his eyes more glazed than ever.

"I'll see what I can do," said the Natterjack, "but it's 'ighly h'improbable."

"And if not," said Jo, with a mock-sentimental face, "let's bear it cheerfully, and keep each other green in memory's garland!"

"And we can always reread the book," added Roger.

"Don't forget to write it," said Ann. "*Little Women,* it's called."

"*Little Women!*" said Jo. "What a good idea. I'll think it over."

Ann held the sprig of golden thyme, and they all whiffed. Maybe it was because the Natterjack tried hard, or maybe it was because Ann loved the March family so. In any event, though the magic didn't manage to arrange a stopover, it did sort of overlap for a moment.

So that although Ann and Roger and Eliza and Jack found themselves back in the twentieth century on a sunny day in July, yet through the windows of the little brown house they could still see the March family, gathered about a wintry fire in the parlor. Beth must have recovered from her cold and Amy come back from visiting Aunt March, for they were present, too. Jo was reading aloud from one of her stories, while Meg sewed a fine seam, Amy touched up a watercolor, and Beth sprinkled her flowers and hummed a hymn tune sweetly under her breath.

For a moment the bright picture hung on the air. Then it wavered and vanished. Ann looked down. In one hand she held the coffee tin with the now toadlike Natterjack; in the other were a few strands of golden thyme that she must remember to put back in the bank when she got home. She and Jack and

Roger and Eliza turned regretfully from the window. They went slowly to old Mrs. Whiton and the car, where once again they sat by the curb. Old Mrs. Whiton did not seem to have minded waiting.

"Well?" she said. "Was it interesting?"

"Yes," said all four children at once.

"I thought perhaps it might be," said old Mrs. Whiton. And flinging one arm wildly out in a left-turn signal, she started the motor and turned the car into the traffic that was homeward bound.

5

Common Time

"I miss Mother," said Ann.

"Not that she doesn't write," put in Roger quickly. "Almost every day."

"I know," said Eliza, with sympathy. "Only the letters you get never tell about the things you want to hear, do they?"

"Ours are mostly about rehearsals," said Ann.

"They haven't had time to look at the Tower of London yet," said Roger.

"Ours are mainly weather," said Eliza. "It's still foggy in London."

The three children were sitting on the beach. Some days had passed since the one they spent in old Concord with the March family. July was lengthening into August, and that time had come that you all know only too well, when everything stops growing, and the leaves hang heavy, and no birds sing, and even the most ideal vacation takes on a certain sameness. And the thought of summer ending and school beginning again would be almost welcome, if it weren't so utterly unthinkable and horrible.

Later on the summer usually picks up, but the time I mean always comes along sooner or later, in the middle, and it has to be lived through.

"What would *you* do in London," said Ann, "if you were there? Besides the Tower of London and where the Bastables lived, I mean."

"Look at the Queen," said Eliza, promptly.

"Watch them changing the guard at Buckingham Palace," said Roger. "What would you?"

Ann thought. "I guess just see Mother," she said. There was a silence.

"Well?" said Eliza. "Why don't we? Why don't we go there and do them *all?*"

"Could we?" said Roger.

And then Jack came out from a solitary swim and joined them on the sands, and they had to start over with explanations.

"I don't see why not," said Jack, when all had been unfolded. "We could think ourselves there, the same as any other place." For in spite of his meeting with the teenage Marches, he still refused to use the word *magic* about the adventures.

"But it wouldn't be a time-wish, exactly, would it?" puzzled Roger. "It'd be more *space*. We've never tried before to go to a time that it's the same time as it is here," he went on, not very clearly, but everyone knew what he meant.

"But it isn't," said Jack. "It's a different time there in London right now. They put the clocks back. Or forward. I forget which. Anyway, it doesn't matter. All time is the same, really."

This was getting too difficult for Ann, and Jack tried to explain.

"It's a new theory. Suppose you were up in an airplane."

"I wouldn't be," said Ann, who preferred keeping both feet on the ground.

"*Suppose* you were. You could look down and see us, here on this beach, and you could see the Boston road, over beyond the woods, too. But it'd take *us* half an hour to walk from here to there. Time's like that. It's all there, Henry the Eighth and Lincoln and yesterday and today, all happening over and over all the time. Only it *takes* time to get from one to the other. Do you see?"

"No," said Ann.

"What *I* want to know," said Eliza, "is how can I get up in that airplane and have it all at once!"

"You can't," said Jack.

"You can if you have a Natterjack," said Roger.

Everyone had been so busy arguing that everyone had forgotten about the wish. Now with one accord the four children rose from the sand, clambered up the rock stairway and ran for the thyme garden. They found the Natterjack and all started talking at once.

But the Natterjack, when it had sorted out what they wanted, looked doubtful.

"That's a 'ard wish, that one there is," it said. "I don't know if it's h'in me to h'accomplish it."

"But we *deserve* a hard one!" said Eliza. "We've been doing all *kinds* of good turns!"

"Not so many last time," said Roger. "It was Jo and the Natterjack did them mostly."

"I washed all those dishes," Eliza reminded him. "Stacks and stacks there were!"

"And I," said Ann shyly, "told Jo to write *Little Women*."

"And that'll be a good deed to the whole world for untold centuries," said Eliza triumphantly. "So you see?"

"Just try," Jack urged the Natterjack. "It'll be simple." And he started telling it all about being up in the airplane and all time going on at once.

The Natterjack regarded him coldly. "Some people," it remarked, "are so smart they'd teach their grandmother to suck h'eggs!"

"Oh, you know about that theory?" said Jack. "I thought it was new."

"Know about it?" said the Natterjack. "I h'*invented* it! Notwithstanding which," it went on, "I 'aven't made a wish that wasn't a New h'England wish in longer than I like to remember. H'it'll take some thinking h'out."

It thought, and the four children watched.

"Common time," it announced after a bit, "that's what's wanted. Time that's common to h'everybody. Common thyme with an 'h' would be the plant required, an' that don't grow in this 'ere garding. Nothing that's common *does*," it added, rather smugly.

"Couldn't we find some?" said Eliza.

"As to *finding* it," said the Natterjack, "nothing could be h'easier. You'll *find* it in the kitchen garding with the rest of the salad stuffs. But as to what you'll do with it when found, you're on your h'own. What goes on in kitchen gardings is no concern of mine. I wouldn't stoop to it." And it started hopping away.

"Wait!" cried Eliza. "You can't desert us at a time like this."

"Why not?" said the Natterjack. "You know 'ow to get h'in an' out now. D'you suppose I've nothing better to do than tag along h'every time? D'you suppose *your* h'adventures are the h'only ones I 'ave to keep track of?"

The four children had never thought of this before. They thought about it now. As for the Natterjack, it hopped into a drift of the woolly-leaved thyme, pulled a few strands over its face for all the world like a woolly counterpane, and went to sleep.

"It isn't coming with us," said Ann.

"We'll have to do it by ourselves," said Roger.

Everybody hesitated. Everybody, that is, but Eliza.

"So much the better," she said, tossing her head. "We can be free as air, without a lot of hindering advice. Come on."

The four children went through the boxwood hedge, past the sundial, along the flower borders, now heavy with hollyhocks and drowsy with hummingbirds, around the house and past the kitchen.

But at the kitchen door Mrs. Annable appeared, with the message that Jack was wanted on the phone. He went in the house while the others waited, fidgeting. Pretty soon he came out again.

"It was Candy Drake," he said (for that was the appetizing name of a new teenage girl he had just met). "She wants me to come over. She's got some new dance records. A lot of the kids'll be there."

"Well?" said Eliza coldly. "Don't you *want* to see Mother?"

It was pitiful to watch the struggle in the face of the hapless youth. At last the call of the teenager won over the lure of enchantment in the soul of Jack. As usual, he veiled his regrets with a show of contempt. "Have fun," he said. "Play your magic games. I've got better things to do." And he started along the cliff in the direction of Candy Drake's house, walking fast and not letting himself look back.

" 'The shadows of the prison world begin to close around the growing boy,' " quoted Eliza.

"Let him go. It's his loss," said Roger.

And he and Eliza and Ann went into the kitchen garden.

In its brick-walled enclosure grew tomatoes and carrots and onions and peas and pepper and squash vines and mint, surrounded by a border of chives and a lower, gray-green plant, stiff and erect, not flat and creeping like the blossomy mounds in the garden on the bank. But after the three children had cautiously smelled, and Eliza had nibbled its holiday-tasting leaves, all agreed that it could only be common, or kitchen, thyme.

"I feel naked without the Natterjack," said Ann.

"I feel poised on the brink," said Roger.

"Pooh. We know what to do," said Eliza. "Rub and whiff, the same as always."

"Better say our wish first, to let the magic know," said Roger, "so there won't be any mistake."

"I want us to be with Mother," said Ann.

"I want us to be with *my* mother, too," said Eliza.

Nobody put in anything about wanting to be in London, because where else would their mothers be?

Roger broke off a stalk of the gray-leaved plant and rubbed it, and they all breathed in.

A second later the three children stood looking around them in utter surprise.

"This doesn't look like any part of London I ever heard of," said Eliza.

"What happened?" said Ann. "Did the play go on tour?"

"It couldn't," said Roger. "It hasn't opened yet."

"The magic must have gone bad," said Eliza. "The thyme wasn't common enough. It took us somewhere else by mistake."

The three children were standing on hot yellow sand, and around them palm trees were tropically grouped. A hot round sun was poised directly overhead, and in the middle distance on all sides waves were breaking.

"It's an island," said Roger. "In a Southern sea, from the look."

"Castaways on a coral isle!" said Eliza. "That's better than nothing, isn't it? Let's make the most of it!"

"I want to see Mother," said Ann stubbornly.

But neither their mothers nor anyone else was to be seen. Then suddenly Roger pointed. "Look!" he said.

What he was pointing at was a column of smoke that was rising from a far part of the island.

"At least it's inhabited," said Eliza, "and not desert."

"Yes, but by what?" quavered Ann.

"Let's find out," said Roger resolutely. And the three children started off in the direction of the smoke column, Ann hanging back only a little. As they drew nearer, they noticed four shapes sticking up against the horizon that were different from the surrounding palms.

"What are those funny-looking trees?" Ann wondered.

"They're not trees, they're totem poles," said Eliza.

"They're not either," said Roger, after a few more steps. "They're people!"

"It's four children," said Ann. "What are they doing up there, pole climbing?"

"Shush!" said Eliza. "Look down below."

The three children stopped short.

An unusual tableau met their gaze. Stretched out on the sand lay a whole tribe of bead-clad natives, taking a midday nap, or siesta. In the center of the group a caldron bubbled over a fire, and that was where the smoke came from. And to one side of the caldron four children hung aloft, tied to spears that had their pointed ends stuck in the sand.

"It's cannibals!" hissed Eliza. "And captives! We must have been sent to rescue them! The magic must have stopped off here on the way, for us to get our good deed over first!"

Three of the four trussed-up children seemed to be peacefully sleeping, but the fourth and smallest was awake. Now she looked down at them, and Ann clutched Roger.

"Where have we seen that little girl before?"

"I don't know," said Roger. "She does look sort of familiar."

"I don't seem to see her very clearly," said Eliza.

"Don't you?" said Roger. "I do."

"Hello," called the little girl suddenly. "My name's Martha. Who are you?" And then Ann knew.

But what she knew seemed so impossible that for a second she couldn't take it in.

The others were talking, introducing each other and asking questions.

"We're caught by cannibals," said the little girl. "Did you come to save us?"

"Yes," said Roger. "I guess we must have. Excuse me a minute." For Ann was tugging at his sleeve.

"Don't you see?" she whispered excitedly. "Didn't you hear her say her name's Martha? It's *Mother!* It's Mother when she was a little girl!"

"How could it be?" said Roger.

"I don't know, it just *is,*" said Ann.

"Why not?" said Eliza. "If all time is going on at once, the magic could take the wrong switch, couldn't it? We wanted to be with our mothers, but we didn't say *when!* The magic must have caught up with them way back in the past somewhere!"

"It's possible," admitted Roger. "That would be why we see the little one more clearly, I suppose, if she's *our* mother."

"Yes, and the next-smallest one must be mine. I can see her *lots* plainer!" Eliza was excited now. "And the other two must be Uncle Mark and Aunt Jane! Mother always *said* they had wonderful exciting times together!"

"But they weren't brought up on a South Sea

124

Island!" objected Roger. "They would have mentioned it."

"What are you saying?" called the little girl Martha. "I can't hear up here."

Roger looked up at her. She *did* look like his mother, sort of. And she looked even more like the baby pictures that turned up from time to time in old trunks or his mother's bureau drawers. A warm protective feeling surged through him suddenly. But he proceeded with caution.

"How did you get here?"

"I wished," said Martha. "Only I wished wrong and the cannibals caught me. And then Mark and Jane and Kathie wished, and followed me and got caught, too. We've got a kind of magic."

"Why, so have we!" said Ann, beaming at her.

"I knew it!" whispered Eliza to Roger. "I always *knew* Mother and the aunts and Uncle Mark had magic adventures back in the olden days! Something Mother said once made me think so. This is the most wonderful thing that's happened to us *yet!*"

"We've been having magic adventures all summer," confided Martha. "Only we've never run into any other magic children before. I wonder why it happened now?"

"Shall we tell her who we are?" whispered Ann to Eliza and Roger. "I want to."

"I don't think so." Roger shook his head regretfully. "I think she's too young to stand it."

"Her infant brain would give way," agreed Eliza.

"How old are you?" Ann asked the small (yet later to be so grown-up and wise and motherly) Martha.

"I'm seven years old," said Martha. "I'm in the second grade next year. My teacher's name is Miss Van Buskirk."

"Why, she's younger than I am!" marveled Ann.

At this point there was a stirring among the other pinioned forms.

"Where am I?" said the one who was really Aunt Katharine (and Eliza's mother).

"Who's there?" said the boy who was Uncle Mark.

"It's Martha," said the Katharine one, peering down. "Who in the world is she talking to?"

"Honestly!" said the one who would grow up to be Aunt Jane. "Standing there gossiping at a time like this!" She glared down at Roger and Ann and Eliza. "Who are you?" she said crossly. If you wonder why she was cross, try being tied to a spear on a cannibal island for a few hours, and you may know.

126

A flurry of explanations and introductions followed. The cannibals meanwhile slumbered on, lulled by the music of seven childish voices, all talking at once.

"They're in a magic adventure, too," Martha was babbling happily, "and our magics kind of overlapped. Isn't that interesting?"

"Oh, they are, are they?" said the Jane one, still crossly.

"Yes we are," said Eliza. "Did you think *you* had all the magic in the world?" She had sometimes yearned to talk back to her Aunt Jane when their strong wills clashed in modern times, and this was her chance.

But she and the Katharine one got along beautifully, and were soon deep in a discussion of the things their different magics could do.

"Why," said Katharine, "when you think of it, there're probably hundreds of children in the middle of hundreds of magics, wandering all over the world all the time! It's a wonder we don't meet more often. It's a wonder we don't have collisions! How did you happen to come *here?*"

Roger and Ann and Eliza looked at each other.

Should they tell or shouldn't they? And would anyone, *could* anyone believe them if they did? Luckily
there was an interruption from the strong-minded
Jane.

"Oh, for heaven's sake!" she said. "What is this, a social tea? What does it matter how they got here? The point is, can they get us down?"

More discussion followed. But action spoke louder than words in the soul of Eliza. To dig the point of Jane's spear from its confining sand was the work of but a moment. Jane fell suddenly and heavily to the ground. And if Eliza forgot to warn her on purpose, so that all Jane's wind was knocked out of her, at least Eliza was sorry for it afterwards, and worked over her quickly and helpfully, untying the bonds that held her to the spear. And it would be something to remember secretly in future, whenever Aunt Jane started ordering her around in her purposeful way!

Roger and Ann were busy meanwhile, freeing the others. "How did you get on this island in the first place?" asked Ann, as the liberated captives sat on the sand, rubbing their chafed wrists and gone-to-sleep hands.

"We were after buried treasure," said Katharine.

"Treasure?" said Eliza, and at the magic word all hearts kindled. "Can we help you find it? Where's it buried?"

Jane and Mark looked at each other and seemed to hesitate. Then Mark nodded. "Follow me," he said. "Better be careful. Walk tiptoe." And he led the others across the sand, explaining as he did so how Martha had been rash and had broken the rules of their magic, and now it had all gone wrong, and he and Jane and Katharine didn't know how they were going to get back to their own time with the treasure, even if they got it dug up and even if they escaped the cannibals.

"How *does* your magic work?" said Jane to Roger. "Maybe it could help. Do you say spells? Or do you have something with you? Some magic coin or something?"

Roger admitted they had *something,* and took the bits of common thyme from his pocket, to make sure they were still safely there.

"It gets us back to our own time when we're finished," said Ann.

"Maybe it'd get *you* back to *yours,* at the same time," said Eliza. "Only it *wouldn't* be the same time, if you see what I mean."

"Clear as mud," said Jane.

"*I* get it," said Mark. "You mean maybe it'd take us back to *your* time with *you,* instead."

"That's what I'm worried about," said Roger. And he repressed an inward shudder.

Because what if it *did* happen like that, and the young Jane and Mark and Katharine and Martha came back with them to modern times? He could think of two ways it might work out. They might take the place of their grown-up selves, and there wouldn't *be* any grown-up Jane and Mark and Katharine and Martha anymore, and that would be awful. Because nice as the small Martha was, as a parent she just wouldn't do.

Or else there Jane and Mark and Katharine and Martha would be, and there their grown-up selves would be, too, and they might bump right into each other. And *that* would be like those horror stories where people go walking down long dark hallways and meet themselves coming in the other direction. And everybody goes mad in the end, and no wonder!

Roger emerged from his thoughts. "You wouldn't like it," he said. "It wouldn't work out. You wouldn't fit in."

And now the boy Mark, who had been studying the sky, pointed out that the sun had started down from high noon and the cannibals would be waking up all too soon, and they had better be digging.

Eliza had been dancing with impatience ever since

the first mention of the treasure, and now as Mark heaved away a flat stone that was half-buried in the sand, she and Jane started scrabbling with their hands in the place where it had been. The others followed suit. Soon the corner of a chest appeared in the ever-widening hole.

"Keep digging," said Roger. "We're getting there."

"Let's get the top uncovered and look in, first," said Eliza. "I can't wait."

And though the boys counseled getting the chest out whole while the getting was good, the strong will of Eliza prevailed (assisted by the strong will of Jane). And at last the four corners of the chest lid appeared.

Jane laid hold of them and pulled. The lid flew back on its hinges. Everybody looked inside.

You all know what pirate treasure is like—the pieces of eight and the diamond necklaces, the emerald bracelets and ruby rings, the topazes and amethysts and gold moidores and all the rest of it. *This* pirate treasure was just what you would have expected, only more so.

"We'll go halves," said Jane.

"Let's start," said Eliza.

She reached for the nearest diamond necklace on

her side, and Jane reached for the nearest similar one on hers. But at that moment a furious cry in native language rent the air.

"Wah! Samoa! Goona goona!" were the words of the cry. Or at least it sounded like that.

Eliza let her diamond necklace fall. Jane never even touched hers. The seven children turned as one, and looked in the direction of the cannibals.

The chief had wakened and was calling his cohorts. Siesta time was over. A hundred savage hands reached for a hundred savage spears and two hundred savage eyes lighted up with joy, hunger and avarice as they saw the children and the treasure. Two hundred feet raced over the sand.

There was only one thing to do.

"Quick!" cried Mark to Roger. "Make the wish! *Any* time's better than this one!"

Roger had hardly a second to do it in. Yet as he rubbed the stalk of common thyme, he managed to think a long careful wish. *Make it be like the time with Jo and Meg and Laurie,* he thought. *Take them back to their own time and us to ours. Please.*

Ann and Eliza leaned with him to sniff the Thanksgiving-y scent. Jane and Mark and Katharine and Martha watched what they did and did likewise.

The next Ann and Roger and Eliza knew, they were in the kitchen garden. Roger poked the gray leaved stalk quickly back into the earth, where it immediately grew again.

Eliza looked around her. "Darn!" she said. "Not only the treasure gone, but those children, too! I *liked* them! Why couldn't we have brought them back with us?"

"We couldn't have kept them," Roger reminded her. "Mother and your mother would have found out sooner or later, and *then* think what would happen!"

Ann and Eliza thought.

"At least we could have played with them all summer!" said Eliza.

Roger looked at her. "They're not *toys!* They have their own lives to lead. It's better this way."

And the others reluctantly nodded.

"I'm going to understand Mother a lot better from now on, though," said Eliza. "Now I know she's been through the mill of the magic, too! And maybe now we know how, we can run into all of them again all the time!"

"Only the *next* time," said Ann, "I'd rather have Mother be just Mother."

And Roger agreed.

6

Time Out of Mind

There was so much to talk over about the island and the treasure and the cannibals that it was at least five minutes before anyone thought of telling the Natterjack. The one who thought of it was Roger, which was typical. As their mother often said, he was the thoughtful one.

The Natterjack, when found (still under its counterpane of woolly thyme) and prodded (by Eliza) and reported to (by all three children talking at once), looked grave.

"H'I *thought* it might 'appen that way," it said.

"Difficult thing, common time. Not h'exclusive at all. Traffic gets crowded. Still, it was worth making the h'effort."

"And now you'll have to think of something else, won't you?" said Eliza.

The Natterjack gave her a look. "H'I don't 'ave to do *anything*," it said. "I may possibly *try*, should the h'occasion h'arise!"

"Humph!" said Eliza. "If the garden's as magic as you say it is, you could try right now. The afternoon's still young. You could just tell it to take us to our mothers right this minute, and no nonsense!"

"I could," admitted the Natterjack.

"It'd be duck soup to it," said Eliza.

"And *you*," said the Natterjack, "might h'end up in a stew! These things aren't so h'easy as all that. I'll 'ave to study the rules. It all 'as to be done according to 'Oyle, and that takes time."

"Here, then," said Eliza, pulling up a tuft of the woolly-leaved thyme and holding it out.

The Natterjack puffed itself up and its eyes seemed to send forth sparks. Ann and Roger and Eliza were reminded suddenly of its dragonlike behavior on the day it reformed the Concord kidnappers.

"Put that thyme back," it said. "You don't know

where it might go! Any more tampering with this 'ere garding," it went on sternly, "and it's the h'*end!*"

Eliza rather shamefacedly replanted the woolly tuft. She knew (sometimes) when she had gone too far.

The Natterjack relaxed a bit, but its tones were still grim. "It might h'interest you to know," it said, "that if you 'ad rubbed that there at this moment, you'd 'ave ended up on a sheep farm in Australia in the year nineteen twelve. And little would 'ave been gained by h'anybody." It yawned. "And now leave me in peace. I've h'unfinished business to take care of."

"But you'll be working on it?" said Roger. "You'll be thinking of ways for us to see Mother?"

"I may," said the Natterjack, "and I may not." And the three children had to be contented with that. (But Eliza was not contented.)

Later that day Jack came home from his party of pleasure at Candy Drake's house, and of course he had to be told about the events of the afternoon. He was interested, not so much in what had happened, as in future possibilities.

"This is keen," he said. "If you could tune in on Mother and the others that way, we can pick them up again at all kinds of interesting times. Like when Uncle Mark made the touchdown for Harvard. Or when Pop proposed to Mother at the Umpty Six Formal!"

"Who cares about things like that?" said Eliza. "It's more of their magic adventures I want to see. And all the *other* magic children we might run into! We might find the *Phoenix and the Carpet* ones! Or that boy in *The Midnight Folk* the night he went to the witches' meeting and met Rollicum Bitem! Now we know about common thyme we can use the kitchen garden every *day,* and the Natterjack won't ever even have to know!"

Roger shook his head. "It wouldn't work."

"Why not?" said Eliza.

"I don't know. I just know it wouldn't. It would be repeating, and we never have, so far. It's as if there were doors into the magic, sort of, and you can only use each one once. Anyway, that's what I think."

"Bushwah," said Jack. "At least we can try. Let's go try now."

"Well, not *right* now," said Eliza. "Maybe tomorrow."

"Scared?"

"Of course not. It's just . . ." Eliza left her sentence

unfinished. She turned and wandered away into the house and upstairs to her bedroom. She wanted to be alone.

"What do you say we go for a walk on the beach?" said Roger to Ann.

"All right," said Ann. And they started down the stairway in the cliff.

Finding himself *by* himself, Jack made a move in the direction of the kitchen garden. Then he stopped. What was the matter with him, worrying about magic plants and talking toads and things that couldn't possibly be true? That day in Concord with the March girls was all a dream. Probably. Or else there was some scientific explanation.

"How childish can you get?" said Jack to himself. And he went into the house to telephone Mary Lou Luckenbill.

Eliza meanwhile sat in her bedroom and thought.

I hope the thoughts *you* have been having about Eliza have not been too harsh. She was really not so bossy and forward and pert and impossible as she all too often seemed. It was the way she was made. Not enough patience had been put in, and too many of those things that your teacher calls "qualities of leadership." To be a leader is all very well when other people follow you, but when they suddenly don't and you find yourself charging off all alone in a wrong direction, it can be shaming. And when you seldom if ever think before you speak, that can be shaming, too, thinking back to it later on.

When Eliza was alone, she was haunted more often than you might believe by the memory of the reckless things she had done here and there during the day. And the echo of her idle boasting would ring loud in her ears and bring a blush to her cheek.

But she was seldom one to admit she was wrong and learn by experience, or to sit back and wait for events to work out by themselves. Perhaps you know someone who is like this.

And if she missed her mother just as much as Ann missed hers, she was not one to admit this, either.

Now, as she sat and thought in her room, she decided to handle the current crisis in a reasonable and restrained manner. She would give the Natterjack three whole days to think up some kind of satisfactory procedure. If it hadn't hit on anything by that time, she would *act*.

And that is exactly how it worked out.

The three days went by without sight of Natterjack,

and the worldly events they contained were pleasant ones, but there was no magic in them.

It was on the afternoon of the third day that Roger and Ann and Jack and Eliza made their seventeenth visit to the thyme garden to see if anything were likely to begin happening, and found that nothing apparently was. The Natterjack, if present, was concealed. The four of them started back to the house. And because they had nothing to do and time hung heavy, they stopped off at the potting shed to bother Old Henry.

Old Henry was busily dealing with early seeds collected from the garden, storing them away in little labeled envelopes, for next season's planting.

"Breathe light," he said. "Chancy things, seeds is." And the four children could see that they were, some being smaller than grains of sand and as easily overlooked, while others were light and thistle-downish, the prey of every passing breeze.

There were store-bought seeds, too, lying in tantalizing packets on the shelf, and Eliza stood turning these over idly. The lettering on one of them caught her eye. She gasped. Then, almost before she knew it, she had slipped the small brown envelope into her pocket. Old Henry and the others didn't seem to have noticed.

"Come on," she said, trying to sound nonchalant. "Let's go sit on the cliff." But there was something in her voice that made the others obey.

"Look!" she went on, when all were established on comfortable rocks. She brought the brown envelope out and pointed.

"Old English Thyme—Mixed," read Roger from the bold capitals at the top, and then, farther down and smaller, "Thompson and Morgan, Ipswich, Suffolk."

"Well?" said Eliza. "If that won't take us to London, what will?"

"It might take us to Ipswich, Suffolk," said Jack. "It might be right across England."

"It won't if I tell it not to," said Eliza. "And if it does, we can catch a train."

"Would seeds work?" Ann wondered.

"Why not? They're the germ of the whole thing. There wouldn't even *be* any garden if it weren't for seeds in the first place! What's more magic than a seed, when you come to think of it? This ought to be the best way yet."

Roger shook his head. "They're stolen property.

Cheaters never prosper. It'd be breaking the rules."

"There comes a time," said Eliza firmly, "when you have to. Anyway, look at that little girl Martha! *She* broke *her* rules, didn't they say, when she ended up on that cannibal island? And look who she grew up to be! You'll just be following your own mother's example!"

"Yes, and remember what happened to her!" said Ann.

"Nothing much *did,* in the end," Eliza reminded her triumphantly. "We came along and saved her. Something always does, sooner or later."

Roger shook his head again. "You can't count on that. Anyway, she was too young to know better."

"If a mere babe could do it," said Eliza, "who are we to be behindhand?"

"How'll we start?" said Jack. "Rub and whiff, same as usual? Only seeds wouldn't have any fragrance, would they? Maybe we ought to taste them."

"Stop encouraging her," said Roger.

Jack looked sheepish. "I'm kind of curious. I want to see if it'd work. Not that it matters. It's all just imagination. Probably."

Ann got up purposefully. "I'm going to find the Natterjack."

"Tattletale!" said Eliza.

"I don't think so," said Roger, getting up, too. "I don't think it comes under that heading at all. We're just saving you from your baser instincts."

"Come on. Hurry," said Ann. And she and Roger ran for the thyme garden.

"Quick, before they get there!" cried Eliza. "How'll we do it?"

"Wish first, and then try a little of everything," advised Jack.

"All right," said Eliza. "I wish we were in London right now."

Jack tore open the brown envelope. Tiny seeds rolled out into his palm. He and Eliza rubbed some between their hands (spilling quite a few that later came up and bloomed in the rock crevices and Old Henry never knew how they got there). They sniffed the fragrance, which was more like dust and old dried leaves than anything else. They tasted a few (and found them the reverse of succulent). The next moment London was all around them.

They knew it was London from the bustle and the noise and the crowds, and from the Tower that graced the background (only not near enough for Eliza to take a good look yet) and from the street cries that resounded in Cockney accents on every hand, "Sweet lavender" and "Cherry ripe, ripe, ripe" and "Shrimps h'all alive, oh!"

But it wasn't the London they had in mind at all. The men that thronged its streets were decked out in doublets and hose and pointed beards; the women wore long skirts and kirtles. The buildings were old and gabled and queer, and yet familiar from pictures in *Master Skylark* and *The Prince and the Pauper.*

"What happened?" said Jack.

"It's that seed," said Eliza. "It said *old* English!"

"And it said 'mixed thyme,'" Jack remembered, "and it *did!* It mixed the centuries."

"Who cares?" said Eliza, looking around her with wide eyes. "This is keen!"

But now the lavender sellers and the cherry vendors and the shrimp merchants were looking at *them,* and first one and then another began to titter and point, until the whole crowd was roaring with laughter.

Jack and Eliza looked at each other, and then down at themselves. And then they knew why.

Up to now the four children had never had to worry about their modern clothes when thyme-traveling. The magic had arranged all that. So far no one

145

had noticed a thing. But now Eliza had broken the rules, and the magic was not prepared to be so accommodating. And there she and Jack were, in the middle of old-time London, Jack in his best Bermuda shorts and sports jacket, and Eliza in a faded yellow cotton dress and ankle socks, and *everybody* was noticing.

"See the great boobies all part naked in the street!" said one.

"Mayhap they fell in the Thames," said another, "and their garments shrank!"

Jack blushed and edged behind Eliza, scrooching down and trying to make his Bermudas come as low on his legs as possible, but Eliza brazened it out. "You'd think," she said, "nobody had ever seen knees before!" And she glared haughtily at the crowd. Luckily at this moment there was a distraction.

A company of people was issuing from one of the buildings nearby. Surrounded by a crowd of gentlemen in peacock colors walked a stately lady in a wide farthingale, a jeweled stomacher, and an immense ruff. The face above the ruff was painted and its nose was sharp. Hair of the brightest red completed the picture. Neither Jack nor Eliza needed to be told who the lady was, particularly when all the onlookers took off their caps, and some knelt, and the air rang with cheers and huzzas.

And any doubts they might yet have were stilled when the lady encountered a mud puddle in her path and stopped short, turning to the bearded gentleman on her right.

"Well, Sir Walter?" she said, smiling grimly. "Have you forgotten your manners? You were more prompt in younger days!"

The bearded gentleman looked rebellious. Then he covered his annoyance with a smile. "Madam, will you walk?" he said. And taking off his fine cloak (not without a glance of regret for its rich velvet and its satin lining), he spread it over the mud for the lady to tread upon, while all the people cheered louder than ever and cried, "Long live good Queen Bess! Long live Sir Walter Raleigh! Long live the ancient courtesye!"

"You wanted to look at the Queen," muttered Jack in Eliza's ear. "Take a good look."

And Eliza did, not at all put out by the fact that the Queen had seen her now and was taking a good look at *her.*

" 'Sblood!" cried good Queen Bess. "What manner of savage is this that stands before the Queen's presence with her nether limbs exposed?"

Eliza had been thinking what to say. Now she said it. "O Queen," she said, "we are strangers come from a far land in our native dress to do you homage."

The Queen's eyes narrowed. "What far land would that be? Not hated Spain?"

"Nay," said Eliza. "We come from America."

The Queen turned to the bearded gentleman, who was busy trying to clean the worst mud from his cloak. "What say you, Sir Walter? Does this wench resemble the natives of your far wilderness of the potato and the tobacco?"

"Not one bit," said Sir Walter. He eyed Eliza shrewdly. "If you are an American, where's your beads and feathers? Where's your wampum?"

Jack felt he had been silent too long. "Wampum," he said, stepping forward, "is a thing of the past. We come from the United States, only they haven't happened yet. We come from the future."

A murmur of disbelief ran through the crowd.

The Queen had not noticed Jack before, and now her eyes dwelt with approval on his youthful frame.

She did not seem to mind the knees. "Interesting," she said, "if true." She turned to her companions. "The lad is well-favored, though the lass is a plain enough wench."

Eliza sputtered with indignation, but before she could speak a scholarly-looking gentleman had appeared at the Queen's elbow. "A likely story!" he said. "They are undoubtedly Spanish spies, sent to do harm upon your majesty's person."

"Not necessarily," said the Queen, regarding him coldly. "There are more things in heaven and earth, Master Francis Bacon, than are dreamt of in your philosophy."

"Francis Bacon?" said Eliza, jiggling up and down excitedly. "I've heard of you. People say you wrote Shakespeare!"

"*Who* says so?" cried the gentleman angrily. "I never!"

"Good," said Eliza. "*That's* settled, then."

"Silence!" roared the Queen, glaring, at them both. "Hold your tongue, you bold-faced jig! Stand still! Speak when you're spoken to!"

"'And don't twiddle your fingers all the time,'" said Eliza. But she didn't say it aloud.

"Now then," said the Queen, returning to Jack and assuming friendlier tones. "How call they you in this future world you say you inhabit?"

"My name's Jack," said Jack.

"A good old English name," approved the Queen.

"And she's Eliza," said Jack.

"Oho!" said the Queen, bending a more favorable look upon that young lady. "So my fame has traveled even to your far time, has it? She was named for *me*, of course?"

"Not exactly," said Jack, who was a truthful boy. "She was named for Great-aunt Eliza Tompkins."

"But *she* might have been named for you, like as not," said Eliza quickly. "All kinds of modern things are."

"Why, sure," said Jack, getting the idea. "We call this whole century the Elizabethan Age. My English teacher says it was just about the best age ever!"

"True. True," said the Queen, looking around her with utter self-satisfaction.

"One of the greatest ships we have is called the *Queen Elizabeth*," said Eliza.

"Only fitting and proper," nodded the Queen. "Go on."

"Well, there's Elizabeth, New Jersey," said Eliza, who was beginning to run out of Elizabeths.

"And Elizabeth Taylor," put in Jack.

"Two noble ladies of your century, I presume," said the Queen. "I am delighted to hear it." She raised her voice and addressed the crowd. "I am satisfied that these brats speak the truth. What they have told me of their times has convinced me. And very sensible times they seem to be, with a proper regard for their glorious ancestry! Let us give them a royal welcome. The lad looks ripe for the palace guard. Take him away and outfit him suitably."

"Lucky you," said Eliza enviously to Jack. "We wanted to see them changing the guard at Buckingham Palace, and now you'll be *in* it!"

"Our palace," Queen Elizabeth corrected her, "is called Whitehall."

"That's OK by me," said Jack. "No skin off my neck either way." And a crowd of handsome young men (who all seemed to be splendid fellows) led him away, clapping him on the back and welcoming him to their stalwart company.

"As for the wench," went on the Queen, "let her be carried back to Whitehall as she is, short kilts and all. With her outlandish rig and her fantastical tales of the future, she should afford us more sport than a whole gaggle of court jesters."

Eliza was not at all sure she liked the comparison. But when spirited steeds were brought and she was helped to mount one, and when she galloped away through the streets of London behind the fabled Queen, her heart sang high. And the fact that a gentleman rode on each side of her (and kept strict watch to see that she didn't turn out to be a Spanish spy after all) only added to the excitement. And the way the people lined the streets and shouted and threw their caps in the air made Eliza feel almost as though it were *she* they were cheering, and not that other Elizabeth. She bowed to the right and left in what she hoped was a regal way, and blew kisses to the crowd. And then they were at Whitehall.

As a palace it was not so dusty. The rooms, while not of Emerald City splendor, were big and impressive, and the courtiers who thronged its halls were handsome as heroes of romance and blazing with gems and satin (only none blazed so brightly as Queen Elizabeth herself).

Eliza followed the Queen into the throne room

and stood at her right hand. Hardly was Her Majesty seated when a young man even more richly dressed than the average strode into the room and knelt before her, kissing her hand.

"Ha!" said the Queen. "You are late, Robin."

"A thousand pardons, dear Gloriana!" said the young man. "And a pox on the cursed business that kept me from your side a single moment!"

"Humph!" said the Queen. "You have missed prime sport by not attending us sooner. Behold, an envoy from the future has descended upon us with rare news of things to come. How say you, Milady Posterity?" She turned to Eliza. "Is the name of Milord of Essex famous in your far time also?"

Eliza wrinkled her forehead. "I've heard *something* about him," she said, "but I can't remember just what."

"Oho!" said the Queen, and Eliza thought she sounded pleased. "You have not heard, for example, that he married his sovereign and became king to reign with her?"

"Oh no!" said Eliza. "I'm sure it wasn't anything like that. You never married anybody. They call you the Virgin Queen."

"And so they jolly well ought to!" said the Queen, complacently.

The face of the young man fell. If he hadn't been such a splendid young gentleman, Eliza would have said that he pouted. The Queen looked at his face and laughed.

"Cheer up, Robin-a-bobbin!" she said. "You know you are king in my heart. Is not that sufficient?"

The handsome young man quickly put on an adoring smile. "To be sure, it is more than enough, dear Gloriana!" he said (but Eliza did not think that he meant it).

"That's my Robin Goodfellow!" said the Queen, putting out her hand. The handsome young man pressed it between his own hands ardently.

It was at that moment that Eliza remembered suddenly what she had heard about Robert Earl of Essex. And as so often happened with Eliza, she spoke her thought aloud without pause for consideration.

"If you like him as much as all that," she said, "why do you cut his head off later?" A second after she had said it she wished she hadn't.

And well she might. The Earl of Essex turned pale and dropped the Queen's hand as though it had burnt him. The Queen turned even paler than he, and her eyes glittered. The courtiers who were near enough to hear whispered together, and some giggled.

Then the scarlet of anger swept over the Queen's face, and she boxed Eliza's ears in a most unqueenly way.

"'Sblood!" she cried, in an awful voice. "What treason is this? Who told you to say those words?"

"Nobody," said Eliza, in a small voice. "It's true. I read it in a history book."

"I don't believe you," said the Queen. "It's a plot to drive my Robin from my side. I don't believe you are a visitor from the future one bit!"

"Probably a witch," said Sir Walter Raleigh.

"Or a traitress in the pay of my enemies," said Milord of Essex, beginning to recover from the shock.

"Or a spy of hated Spain, just as I said," said Master Francis Bacon.

"Away with her to the Tower!" cried the Queen. "Let her cool her heels in a prison cell till I make up my mind what to do with her. She shall be burnt or beheaded or both, as a warning to all who would harm my Robin-a-bobbin! Guards, ho!"

A score of guardsmen surged forward.

"I take it back!" cried the wretched Eliza. "It

probably isn't going to happen at all! I probably got it wrong! I never *was* very good in history! Ask my teacher!"

"Aha!" cried the Queen. "So you have a 'teacher,' do you? I *thought* you were over-young for such miching mallecho without *some* prompting! Mayhap a taste of bread and water and solitary confinement will help you to remember your 'teacher's' name! Take her away!"

Strong arms seized Eliza and began marching her the length of the throne room.

"Don't worry," breathed a shaky voice in her ear. "We wanted to see the Tower of London, didn't we? Now we will."

Eliza looked up and met the familiar gaze of Jack, as he moved along at her side with the rest of the Queen's guard. She had never been so glad to see her brother in her life.

"Thank heavens!" she said. "I'd forgotten all about you!"

But apparently the Queen had forgotten about him, too, and now she remembered. For at this moment her voice rang out.

"Nay! Stay! Halt!"

The guards halted.

"Let the lad who calls himself Jack be arrested immediately and brought to my council chamber. I would question him in private," commanded the Queen.

"Too bad, old chap," said the guardsman on Jack's left, laying a hand on his shoulder.

"Here. Don't worry about me. Save yourself," hissed Jack to Eliza, shoving something into her hand.

"No fraternizing with the prisoner. Sorry, old man," said the guardsman on Jack's right, taking him by the elbow and turning him around.

And Jack was marched away in one direction and Eliza in another, out of the throne room and through the corridors of Whitehall. Her escort paused at a doorway. Flunkies sprang to open it. Outside a flight of broad stone steps led downward. At their foot lapped the waters of the River Thames. A black and sinister-looking barge stood moored and ready for any who were to make the fatal journey Towerward.

As Eliza stepped onto the barge she unclenched her hand and looked at what Jack had thrust into it. It was the packet of thyme seed.

But before she could do more than read the words "English Mixed," the barge swung with the tide, jolting her, and the packet fell from her fingers. A puff of wind caught it and bore it aloft for a second. Then it fluttered down to the surface of the river and sailed away out of sight, carrying its precious cargo of safety with it.

A sob was heard. Whether it was Eliza's, I will not say. Perhaps it was the remorseful wind.

"Cheer up, little lady. All may yet be well," said a kindly guardsman. But Eliza didn't hear. And she didn't look at the banks of the Thames slipping past, or see the grim fortalice of the Tower draw nearer, or notice the Traitors' Gate as they went through it.

Eliza was in despair.

7

The Last Time?

"I hope the Natterjack's there," panted Roger to Ann, as they raced for the thyme garden. "If it's still disappeared, we'll never find it before it's too late!"

"Where do you suppose it goes in between whiles?" panted Ann to Roger.

"Sort of merges into things generally, I suppose," said Roger. "Like protective coloring, only more so."

"I hope it's un-merged now," said Ann. After that they had no breath left for anything but running.

Luckily the Natterjack proved to be in residence. It was sitting, as usual, upon the sundial. Roger wasted no precious seconds in words. Picking it up, he raced back toward the cliff, while Ann, who had got her second wind, babbled excitedly of what had happened.

"H'insubordination!" said the Natterjack, when it heard what Eliza and Jack had done. "I am shocked and chagrined, but 'ardly surprised. Just when I 'ad worked out the 'ole problem, too!"

"You *have?*" said Roger.

"Good," said Ann. "Maybe we'll be in time to stop them, and we can all go together properly."

But they weren't. When the cliff came into view, no one was to be seen but a chipping sparrow that was investigating the flavor of the Mixed Thyme seed and finding it to its liking (though whether or not it wished and where it went if it did do not come into this story).

"Quick!" said Roger. "If you've figured out how to do it. Let's follow them before they get into trouble!"

"H'it's not so h'easy as that!" said the Natterjack. "Thrown a wrench into the works properly, your clever friends 'ave, meddlin' with their nasty store-bought seed! The thyme is out of joint, Shakespeare. An' 'ighly h'uncomfortable it *is* for it, too! You've 'eard of someone's *nose* being out of joint? Well, for

161

thyme h'it's the same principle, only more so! In the mood that garding's in, if it lets us go back now, h'it may be for the *last time!*"

"I don't care!" said Roger.

"Are you sure?" said the Natterjack. "Think! No more carefree h'adventures, no more comings an' goings through the back o' beyond at your h'own sweet will! No more frolickin' with the calendar as though it was a h'empty mockery!"

"I don't care, either!" said Ann. "We've got to save them!"

"Very well," said the Natterjack, and Roger thought it sounded pleased with them. "'Urry!"

Again there was a mad dash for the thyme garden.

"Set me down," said the Natterjack, as they came in sight of the flowery bank. It gave two hops and settled on a patch of creeping thyme with bright pink flowers. "Thymus 'erba-barona. H'otherwise known as seedcake thyme," it announced. "So called h'after the delicacy of the same name. And what could be more h'English than *that?*"

"I *know!*" said Ann, who had once tasted that horrid concoction of sponge cake and caraway seeds. "Only the English could stand it!"

The Natterjack looked affronted. "H'I don't know what you mean, h'I'm sure!" it said, in its most British voice. "H'excellent tasty stuff, seedcake is!"

"Ugh!" said Ann. And "Ugh!" she said again, as she whiffed the sprig Roger picked, with its aroma reminiscent of dry munchings at teatime.

Roger opened his mouth to wish.

"Careful!" warned the Natterjack. "'Aste makes waste, remember. What were they planning to do in London? Besides visit sundry mothers?"

"Look at the Queen," said Roger.

"Put that in," said the Natterjack. "Put h'everything in!"

"Let me," said Ann. "I remember." She grasped the thyme and hurried on, running her words together in her eager heedlessness. "I wish we'd go to London and look at the Queen and see the Tower and the Nesbit children and our mothers and . . ."

She paused to catch her breath before going on to say just *when* she wanted to see these things and under what circumstances, but the rest of her wish was left unsaid. The magic, always ready to take advantage, took it.

The next Ann and Roger and the Natterjack

knew, they were all three looking at the Queen and the Queen was looking back at them.

But she wasn't the Queen they had expected to see, at all.

"She's not the modern one!" whispered Ann to Roger. "She's old-fashioned. It's gone wrong again!"

Old-fashioned was certainly what the Queen was, from her long stiff black gown to the white lace cap that covered her white hair. She was sitting on a carved rosewood chair in what seemed to be her private chamber, and looking at Roger and Ann with an expression of utter disapproval. The part of them she was looking at was their knees.

"Very shocking," said the Queen.

Ann and Roger looked down at themselves. And then they realized (as Jack and Eliza had before them) that all rules were broken, and there they were in whatever time they were in, still in their modern clothes, and concealment was an idle dream.

"Not only unannounced," went on the Queen, "but unclothed! Such a thing has never happened before! I shall complain to Mr. Gladstone!"

"I certainly should, Ma'am," said one of the two ladies-in-waiting who hovered nearby.

"Mr. Disraeli would never have allowed it!" said the other.

Roger knew what time it was now. "It's Queen Victoria!" he hissed at Ann. "It's the Widow of Windsor!" For he had read the poem of that name by Mr. Rudyard Kipling.

"I am a widow," admitted the Queen, "and Windsor is one of my castles, though this is Buckingham Palace. But your tone is disrespectful, and you seem ill-nurtured."

"Oh, Ma'am!" cried the Natterjack, giving voice suddenly. It seemed to be overcome by some strong emotion. "Oh, Ma'am, forgive these 'apless babes as know not what they do, an' 'ow should they, brought up in barbarous foreign parts an' all? H'accept the 'omage of a loyal, 'umble subjeck! God save h'our gracious Queen!" And it squatted on its back legs and assumed the nearest approach it could to a kneeling position.

The Queen regarded it coldly, unmoved by this effusion. "Talking beasts," she said. "What will these so-called scientists think of next? And some people would call that modern progress, I suppose! As if we had not progressed quite sufficiently already! When I

165

see what my reign has accomplished, I see no need for any further alterations whatsoever! Let well enough alone, I say!"

"I could not agree with you more," said the first lady.

"How true," said the second.

"I 'umbly begs your pardon, Ma'am," said the Natterjack. "I won't say another word, swipe me bob I won't!" And it folded its lips tightly and remained in an abject crouching position before the Queen's chair. Ann thought its feelings were hurt, and gave the Queen an indignant look, but Roger was more diplomatic.

"We won't bother you anymore, Ma'am," he said, trying to sound as respectful as possible. "We'll be going any minute. There's just one thing. Have you seen a boy and girl something like us just lately?"

"I have never seen anything remotely like you before in my life," said the Queen, "and I hope never to again."

"Thanks," said Roger. He turned to the others. "Wrong queen," he said.

"Really!" said the Queen.

"Oh, that's all right," said Roger. "It's not *your* fault. Maybe we'll pick them up at the next stop." He turned back to Ann. "You know, it'd be a lot simpler if you'd just wished to be with Jack and Eliza. Then we wouldn't have to keep trying all these places."

"I don't care," said Ann. "It's more interesting this way. Looking at all the ancient sights."

"Really!" said the Queen again.

"Don't mention it," said Roger. "Good-bye," he added, bowing politely.

"We had an awfully nice time," put in Ann, remembering her manners. She picked up the Natterjack. Roger took the sprig of thyme from her and rubbed it, and they all whiffed.

The next instant three women were alone in a room in Buckingham Palace, staring at the place where two children and a talking toad had recently been.

"We are not amused," said the Queen.

"Neither are we," said the ladies-in-waiting.

While the Queen and her ladies were staring at empty space, Ann and Roger and the Natterjack were staring at the Tower of London. For that had been the next thing in Ann's wish; so of course it was the next stop.

As a tower, it was worth staring at. Its aspect was

historical and its battlements were grim. In short, it was every bit of what it had been cracked up to be.

Several yeomen of the guard stood about, looking as if they had just stepped out of the Gilbert and Sullivan opera of that name.

"Beefeaters, they're called," said Roger.

"They look it," said Ann.

The Natterjack was once more stirred by emotion. "H'I am moved," it said, regarding the Tower. "Oh, 'istory, 'istory! 'Ow 'appy I am h'I'm a Briton!"

There was no sign of Jack or Eliza, but otherwise the approach to the Tower was crowded with sightseers. All were in Victorian dress; so Ann and Roger knew the times had not changed. But they found that if they pressed into the thick of the crowd, no one had space enough to notice their outlandish costume.

At the Tower gate, a tourist-guide was plying his trade.

"Step up, step up!" he cried. "See the Trytors' Gyte. See Sir Walter Raleigh's nyme, where 'e scratched it while langrishin' in durance vile! See the cell of Lydy Jyne Gry!"

"Ow, 'Enry, 'ow grisley!" cried a young lady in a feather boa. "Ow, I *shall* enjoy this!"

All the people crowded forward, and Ann and Roger crowded with them. The magic had not provided suitable currency of the realm, but they kept close to the heels of an exceedingly sizable Victorian family, and the Victorian papa did not seem to notice that he had paid for two extra. The Natterjack, in Ann's pocket, got in free.

The two children (and the Natterjack) followed the sightseers and the sightseers followed the guide, listening to tales of torture and anecdotes of unjust martyrdom till all history seemed a register of crimes and follies and even the Natterjack in Ann's pocket muttered "A truce to gore!" and the young lady in the feather boa said, "Ow, 'Enry, I *am* enjoying this!"

It was in the seventh cell they visited that Ann suddenly had a strange prickly feeling, rather as if her fingers and toes were going to sleep, but not quite. It was more as if they were waking up. She did not want to call attention to herself by asking questions, but she was glad when the Victorian father asked the guide, "Pray, what is the history of this chamber?"

"Not much 'istory to this 'ere," said the guide. "More for the run-o'-the-mill prisoners, it were."

"Children, you need not make a note of this apartment," said the Victorian gentleman to his nine sons and daughters, who had their notebooks and pencils in hand. "No one of any consequence was executed from here. Where is the room where the Princes in the Tower were murdered?" And all the sightseers pushed eagerly on.

Ann's heart had quickened at the words of the guide, and now she plucked at Roger's sleeve and gave him a significant look. As the others left the room, the two children lingered behind.

"They've *been* here!" cried Ann, as soon as they were alone. "Or at least *one* of them has! I feel it in my bones! It's as if the room's trying to speak to me. And look!" Something had caught her eye on the far wall; now she ran to inspect it closer. Someone had scratched letters in the stone.

"E, L, I, Z . . ." read Ann. There the lettering broke off, either worn away by time or because something had interrupted the writer.

"That doesn't signify," said Roger. "There must have been dozens of different Elizabeths shut up in the Tower when you count up!"

"No," said Ann, "it *means* something! I *know* it does! If things could go wrong for us, they could go wrong for *them,* couldn't they? Specially when they broke the rules that way! They prob'ly met a worse queen than we did! She prob'ly sent them to the Tower to be tortured with racks and things! Why, if all time is one, Eliza's prob'ly right here in this room right now, suffering untold agony! Only how do we get through to her?"

"Or *her* through to *us?*" said Roger.

Ann took the Natterjack out of her pocket, and they consulted it. It looked grave.

"That's a 'ard trick, that one is," it said. "Still, as it's the last time, maybe h'it'll be accommodating. Rub your sprig."

Roger rubbed, and the Natterjack muttered to itself. Ann leaned closer to overhear.

"'Ocus pocus!" it was saying. "Come ghoulie, come ghaestie, come long-leggedy beastie! Come, come, Eliza dear, h'out of the h'everywhere into the 'ere!"

"The nerve!" said Eliza, appearing suddenly in their midst. "What if I *am* long-legged? I'm a growing girl! What kept you so long?"

"You poor thing, has it been awful?" said Ann.

"Of course not. It's been fun!" boasted Eliza (but she was not telling the strict truth).

So then of course Roger began scolding Eliza for spoiling everything and making it be their last time, and they all three quarreled and made up again, and told each other about their different adventures and compared queens, and what with the babble of three childish voices all raised at once, it was but a moment before the tourist-guide stuck his head in at the door.

"Visitors are h'asked to remain in a Conducted Group," he told them sternly. "No dawdling, no 'anging be'ind, and speak only in a Low Voice." His eye fell on Eliza. "I 'aven't seen *you* before, Missy, That's one 'alf-price h'admission not paid for." He held out his hand. "Sixpence, please." Then he saw the Natterjack. "That beast must be taken *h'out*," he said. "No pets or h'infants in arms allowed." And he started for the Natterjack purposefully.

"What'll we do?" said Ann.

"Better go back where I came from," said Eliza. "I just remembered. We have to, anyway. We left Jack behind."

"Rub the other way," said the Natterjack, hopping out of reach of the guide's outstretched hand. The guide heard it speak, and stepped back, turning pale.

Roger rubbed the thyme-sprig in the opposite direction, and wished, and they all whiffed.

The next moment the guide stood looking round

an empty room. He turned even whiter, backed to the doorway, and scuttled down the corridor to resign his job and spend the rest of his life writing papers for the Psychical Research Society.

Meanwhile Ann and Roger and Eliza and the Natterjack found themselves still in the same Tower cell, back in Elizabethan times. Nothing had visibly changed, save that Eliza's handwriting on the wall looked fresher, as though she had just left off writing it (as indeed she had).

"Now to find Jack," said Ann.

"Wait," said Roger. "Let's reconnoiter first. We don't want to waste time on any more mistakes."

"I wish we had the old rules back," said Ann. "About people not noticing we're different."

"It'd be even better if they didn't notice us at *all*," said Eliza, "and we could remain anomalous."

"There's another thing," said Roger. "We've forgotten all about doing a good deed."

"We don't have to, anymore," said Eliza. "It won't make any difference, if it's the last time, anyway."

"Don't keep reminding us," said Ann.

"I think we ought to do one, anyway," said Roger. "If it's good-bye to the magic, we might as well part friends."

"Oh, all right," said Eliza. "I don't mind, if it comes up naturally. I'm not going out of my way, looking for one."

"H'if you ask me," the Natterjack joined the conversation, "h'actions speak louder than words. Thyme an' tide wait for no man, and h'even last times don't last forever, you know!"

When Roger took the thyme sprig from his pocket, it *did* look as if it couldn't last much longer. Its pink blossoms were faded and its leaves hung limp.

"Oh dear," said Ann, "and we haven't come to the important part of the wish yet. About Mother!"

But it seemed there was still life in the sprig, for when they all sniffed its caraway redolence and wished to be where Jack was, and when Roger rubbed, right away they *were*.

Where Jack was turned out still to be alone with Queen Elizabeth in her council chamber. He was telling her all about the Twentieth Century, and the three children couldn't tell whether or not the magic was being helpful about children's not noticing, because they were both too absorbed to notice *anything*.

"And then there's television," Jack was saying.

"It's a picture that's sent for hundreds of miles, and it *talks!*"

"'Sblood!" said the Queen. "What words of wisdom does it say?"

"Oh, all kinds of things," said Jack, "and baseball games and shows."

"Like the plays of Will Shakespeare," said the Queen.

"Sort of," said Jack, "only different."

"Marry come up!" said the Queen. "Truly this must be an age of marvels. No witchcraft could invent such wonders. It must verily be a fact that you and your sister come from future worlds!"

"Then let her out of the Tower!" cried Jack.

"All in good time," said the Queen. "From what I have observed of her character, 'twill do her no harm to worry a bit longer. But now mark me. I have an idea. Is it true what she said, that I cut off Milord of Essex's head one day?"

"I'm afraid so," said Jack.

"Alas," said the Queen. "Poor Robin. Still if it must be, why not save time and cut it off *now?* Then *you* could stay with me and take his place as my favorite! With the help of these new inventions you

tell me of, these air ships and this wireless and this speaking vision . . ."

"Television," Jack interrupted.

"Telling vision," the Queen corrected herself. "With the help of these new improvements, which you can show me how to manufacture, I can make Merrie England ruler of the world even sooner than I would have, anyway! What say you, boy?"

Jack hesitated. The thought of being a queen's favorite was not to be sneezed at, and he liked what he had seen of the palace. Then, too, there were several teenage maids of honor about that might be pleasant to know, particularly one small blonde he had noticed, called Lady Samantha Drake. On the other hand, a queen who talked so lightly of cutting off heads did not seem to be the most comfortable kind of queen to be the favorite *of.* And he was not entirely sure that he could construct a really satisfactory television set out of Elizabethan raw materials.

It was at this moment that he looked up, in the direction of Ann and Eliza and Roger and the Natterjack. And because they were all in the same magic adventure together, he saw them all quite clearly. And Ann thought that a relieved expression crossed his face.

"I don't think it would work out," he said. "Thanks just the same."

The Queen's eyes glittered. Too late Jack remembered about women scorned, and he thought that a queen scorned might very likely be even *worse*.

"Not that it wouldn't be keen," he said quickly. "It's just that I have to get home. I've got things to do."

"What things?" said the Queen, coldly.

"Well," said Jack, "there's the Yacht Club race. And the Midsummer Cotillion . . ."

"What are these?" said the Queen. "Trials of skill?"

"Sort of," admitted Jack.

The Queen relaxed, and smiled graciously. "In that case," she said, "you are forgiven. It is not your wish, but your duty that calls you from my side. It is fate that divides us. You have a rendezvous with destiny!"

Some words Jack had read in school popped into his mind. He said them. But not being a poetical boy, he didn't remember them quite right. "I could not love it here so much, loved I not honor more," he said.

"Neatly put," said Queen Elizabeth.

On a sudden inspiration Jack knelt and kissed the Queen's hand. Eliza chose this moment to giggle.

The Queen looked up, and the three children could tell from her expression that she saw them. And yet at the same time she seemed to be looking straight through them, as though they were transparent. Seemingly the magic was being obliging about people's not noticing, and yet not completely so.

"Angels and ministers of grace defend us!" cried the Queen. "What ghostly visitants are these?"

"They're not," said Jack. "They're my friends, come to take me away."

The Queen peered closer. "To be sure," she said, "and your sister is among them. They have freed her. What power these future beings must have, to dare to defy *me!* And how much they could teach me! It hardly seems worthwhile your coming at all, if you're just going to go away again. Oh, stay here with me, all of you, and help me to reign wisely and choose what is best for England! Sometimes it all seems so difficult I wonder why I try to go on!"

Roger looked at Ann and Ann looked at Roger, and each of them knew what their good deed was going to be.

"You just keep it up the way you've been," said Ann. "You're doing fine."

"Remember what we told you about the Elizabethan Age," said Eliza. "Keep on encouraging those poets and playwrights."

"Don't worry about politics," said Roger. "Who do you think brings England together all united and independent of the rest of Europe forever?" For that was what he had read about Queen Elizabeth in his history book.

"Do I do that?" said the Queen.

"Yes," said Roger, "you do."

The Queen looked pleased, but still reluctant for them to depart. "Have you nothing more to tell me?" she asked.

"Don't worry about that Spanish Armada," said Eliza. "It'll be duck soup."

"And don't cut off Lord Essex's head till you absolutely *have* to," said the tenderhearted Ann.

"I won't," promised the Queen.

And now Roger took the poor last shreds of the seedcake thyme from his pocket and rubbed them, and they whiffed and wished.

What happened after that was like the last parts

of a dream, just before you wake up. The rest of the wish came true, but all in a rush and run together in quick flashes that blurred and became something else as soon as they were seen. Maybe it was because most of the thyme was worn away and the parts that were left had to work extra hard and fast to do it at all.

The Queen and the council chamber disappeared, and at first the four children (and the Natterjack) seemed to be rushing through dark empty space. Then it seemed as though the space were sky and they were flying across it. The earth below kept changing its aspect as centuries merged into other centuries. Still they flew. Or was it time that was flying and they who were standing still? Who could tell? Certainly not Ann and Roger and Jack and Eliza.

At one moment something came hurtling toward them. As it drew nearer the four children could see that it was a magic carpet. Riding the carpet, which was stretched out stiffly on the air, were four children and a golden bird that could only be a Phoenix.

"It's the Nesbit children!" cried Ann. "The Phoenix and the Carpet ones! Which adventure do you suppose they're going on?"

But before she or any of the others could call

"Hello," or even wave, the carpet had sailed past and disappeared. And after that things got even faster and more confused.

For a moment they seemed to be standing in a London street, in the present day, to judge from the kind of traffic that was passing. The building they were facing seemed to be a theater, and on it was a sign advertising Ann and Roger's father's play, with an opening date a month away. Two ladies were walking down the street toward the theater. Ann and Roger and Jack and Eliza looked at the ladies. And a great cry of recognition rose from four throats.

But whether the ladies saw *them* or whether their cry fell on deaf ears will never be known.

For at that moment everything blacked out completely, and the *next* moment they and the Natterjack found themselves standing on the edge of the cliff with the waves of the Atlantic beating on the beach below, and it was over.

"Foiled again!" said Eliza.

"And for the last time!" mourned Ann.

"You saw your mothers, didn't you?" said the Natterjack.

"Yes, we *saw* them!" said Jack.

Roger didn't say anything. He started for the

thyme garden. The others followed. Once there, he poked the haggard remains of the seedcake thyme back into the earth.

But nobody stayed to see whether they grew again or not. And nobody spoke as the four children trudged away from the blossomy bank and past the flower borders and across the lawn to the house. Only Ann turned and ran back for a last word with the Natterjack, which as usual had gone about its own business as soon as it reached its familiar garden.

"Good-bye," she said. "Don't think we blame *you*. It's not *your* fault. We know you did your best."

The Natterjack did not reply. It was occupied with a small spider. But Ann thought that it looked gratified.

She ran to join the others, where they sat silently on the front steps of the house.

After a while the silence got to be too much to bear.

"Our mothers looked happy," she said. "They were smiling."

"Yes," said the others.

"The poster on the theater was keen," said Roger.

"Yes," said the others.

There was a silence.

"The rest of this summer," said Eliza, "is going to be *awful*."

The others did not deny this.

"Of course," said Jack, after a bit, "there's the Yacht Club race . . ."

The others gave him a withering look.

"And the Midsummer Cotillion," he went on, nothing daunted. He got up and smoothed down his hair. "I'm going inside," he said. "I'm going to phone Susie Eberly."

And he did.

8

The Time Is Ripe

Of course the rest of the summer wasn't really so awful as Eliza expected, and yet in a way it was. Considered as a time of magic adventure it was an empty mockery, yet for those who could open their hearts to swimming, sailing, picnics and mere idling, it had its jim-dandy side, and the four children found that they could open their hearts quite wide to these most of the time.

But ever and anon the Australian crawl would flag, or an oar would trail listlessly in the water or a hot dog remain uneaten on a paper plate, and Ann and Roger and Eliza would look at each other, and each would know what the other two were thinking.

Jack had less time for repining than the rest of them. To begin with, there was the Yacht Club race, and then there was the terrible decision of whether to take Julie or Janina or Jerry Lou to the Midsummer Cotillion. In the end he took Adrienne.

And so the days of August passed, and white phlox and blue globe thistles stood in the flower borders, and wild asters started blooming along the roadsides and swallows held political meetings on the telephone wires, and the nights began to have a touch of chill in the air.

The four children seldom went near the thyme garden now, but one evening just at sunset Ann found herself there.

Ann was the one who missed the Natterjack most. As she said to the others, even if there weren't going to be any more wishes, it would be nice to see it and say hello once in a while, just for old times' sake.

So this evening she went to look for it, and it wasn't on the sundial; so she went through the opening in the box hedge, and it wasn't there, either, and yet once there she stayed, looking down on the cushiony billows that cascaded to the sea, and breathing the spicy air that was now, alas, but the fragrance of memory.

There weren't so many of the starry blossoms twinkling purple and white and pink and red as there had been in happy days gone by; in fact there were hardly any. Where the flowers had been, each plant wore a fluffy, grayish look. And bending closer, Ann saw that each stem bore a tiny coronet of seed. And some words she had heard in the past echoed in her ears like the sound of a last good-bye. Sadly she turned to go, and met Roger and Eliza, coming through the boxwood hedge.

"What are you doing out here?" said Eliza.

"I don't know. I just came," said Ann.

"So did we," said Roger.

"The thyme is ripe," Ann told them. "It's stopped blossoming. It's got seed."

"Then it would have been over today, anyway," said Roger.

"It makes it all seem more final, somehow," said Eliza. "I kept kind of hoping against hope."

"So did I," said Ann.

Somebody came through the opening in the hedge. It was Jack. He had had small time for the other three in the days that had followed the adventure with Queen Elizabeth. Now he seemed unusually friendly.

"I just thought," he said. "Today's the day the play opens."

"I've been thinking about it all day," said Roger.

"I forgot," said Ann.

"If we could only be there!" said Eliza.

"If we'd managed better, we would be," said Roger.

"It's all my fault!" said Eliza.

"Mine, too," said Jack. "Worse than you, 'cause I'm oldest."

"It's everybody's fault," said Roger. "We should have husbanded our harvest."

"It's like those awful fables," said Ann. "We were grasshoppers and we should have been ants."

There was a silence. In the silence a small figure hopped through the growing dusk and landed at their side.

"You!" said Ann. "I thought you were never coming back."

"I meant you to think so," said the Natterjack.

"How've you been?" said Jack, politely.

"Busy," said the Natterjack.

Everybody tried not to think envious thoughts

about what it had been busy doing, or hopeful ones about what it might do next. The Natterjack waited a long time before it spoke again. It seemed to be enjoying keeping them in suspense.

"Well?" it said at last. "This is the great day, I believe?"

"Yes," said Roger.

"It would be nice to be there, wouldn't it?" said the Natterjack.

"Yes," said Ann.

"Well?" said the Natterjack again. "Why not?"

"But you said last time was the last time!" said Ann.

"I said *maybe* it would be," said the Natterjack. "Never underestimate the power of a magic to change its mind. What would be the good of its being magic in the first place if it couldn't do a simple trick like that? Besides, you did a good turn, didn't you?"

"We tried," said Ann. "But I guess Queen Elizabeth would have done all right without us."

"Modest as well as sensible," said the Natterjack. "You're the best of *this* lot, I always said so."

"I know who the worst is," said Eliza, with a sheepish grin.

"So," said the Natterjack, fixing her with a look, "do h'I. Well? Is h'everybody ready?"

Everybody was.

"Then take your thyme," said the Natterjack.

"Which kind should we pick?" said Roger.

"H'it makes no difference," said the Natterjack. "At a time like this all thyme is the same."

Four hands reached out eagerly and broke off four leafy bits, scattering the tiny seeds to replenish the coming year. Four hands rubbed, four noses sniffed, and four hearts wished. Ann remembered to pick up the Natterjack.

The next instant they were standing in a crowded London street outside the theater they had seen before, and the instant after *that* they were swept into the lobby in the midst of the eager crowd. As they were propelled past the box office, Roger noticed a sign on it that said, "House Sold Out," and felt gratified.

No one spoke to the four children or seemed to see them, and they soon realized that they must be invisible, which, of all ways of going on a magic adventure, is perhaps the most satisfactory.

And it is a particularly convenient way to attend a theatrical performance, also, for one needs no tickets, and may stand wherever one likes without anyone's asking one to take off one's hat, or shouting, "Down in front!"

Furthermore Ann found (when a determined lady bumped into her and then went right on *through*) that not only were they invisible, but they had no weight or substance, either.

When she told her discovery to the others, it was but the work of a moment for the four children to pick out their favorite seats in the house (in the middle of the front row, of course) and sit in them, or rather, upon the laps of those who were there before them.

If you have ever been without weight or substance, you will know that even the boniest knees or the plumpest and most slippery laps are perfectly comfortable. Ann and Roger and Jack and Eliza sat back at their ease, and the people beneath seemed to notice nothing unusual.

But of course the four children could still see each other perfectly clearly, and Eliza had to giggle as she looked at Jack, balanced on the knee of a portly and bejeweled dowager.

And it seemed that, although those below saw nothing and felt nothing, yet in a way the moods of those who were sitting on them got through to them. For when Eliza giggled, the mild little man under her began to giggle, too, and couldn't say why, and was glared at and spoken to severely by his large wife for playing the fool.

And then the lights dimmed, and there was that enchanted moment there always is before the curtain goes up, and then the curtain *did* go up, and all was utter rapt attention in the hearts of the four children. Ann put the Natterjack on her shoulder where it could see.

The first scene in the play was a short one, a sort of prologue, and it was a little slow in getting under way. Also, it was a hot night and the theater was stuffy. Some of the audience began to stir restlessly, and several people coughed. One of the nicest lines was said, and hardly anybody laughed. Ann and Roger and Jack began to feel worried.

Eliza felt worried, too, but then she began to think. Among the few people who had laughed at the funny line were she and Ann and Roger and Jack. That was only to be expected. That was only loyal. Besides, it was a funny line.

But the only *other* people who had laughed had been the four people sitting under them. And Eliza,

always one for putting two and two together, re-membered how the little man beneath her had gig-gled, before, when *she* had giggled. And she had an idea.

As soon as the first short scene was over, she told her idea to the other three.

"It's *us!*" she told them. "We're contagious! It's like spirit mediums. We little know the power we wield!" And the others saw the logic in her words.

In the brief pause before the curtain rose again they held council, and decided what to do. Then they separated. Ann took the front rows and Eliza took the back ones. Jack took the dress circle and Roger the gallery.

When the second scene began, they proceeded ac-cording to plan. Each one sat down upon the first person in the first row of his particular section, stayed there for a minute or two, thinking happy, enthusi-astic, appreciative thoughts all the while, and then moved onto the lap of the person in the next seat, and so on, all across the row. When one of them finished a row, he started on the one behind. As Eliza said afterwards, it was like the collection plate in church.

And as the four emissaries of delight moved through the audience, the spirit of happy, enthusi-astic appreciation moved through it, too, till the air rang with laughter and applause.

"A hit, a very palpable hit!" said a critic in the sixth row, as Ann abandoned her perch on his knee.

"Too, too delicious!" cried a lady in the dress circle, hitting the gentleman with her with her fan.

"Ow, 'Enry, 'ow lovely!" cried an old, old lady in a feather boa, in the gallery. "Ow, I *am* enjoying this!" And Roger wondered fleetingly if they had met before, years and years ago, in the Tower of London.

In the interval after the first act the four children haunted the lobby and eavesdropped, hearing none but the most ecstatic comments. Eliza kept looking for Ann and Roger's father, but he was nowhere to be seen.

"He'll be roaming the streets," said Roger, "and Mother'll be in her hotel room. They couldn't endure the suspense."

When the bell rang for act two, the children decided the audience needed no further warming up. Anyway, the play was so good that people couldn't help enjoying it, now they were in a mood to. So Ann and Roger and Jack and Eliza reassembled in the front row, and sat enthralled until the end.

And at the end there were seventeen curtain calls and cheers for all the actors and cries of "Author! Author!" None shouted louder than Eliza.

At last the father of Roger and Ann appeared on the stage, looking rumpled and confused as if he'd just been dragged in from roaming the streets, which was probably true.

And he made a slightly mumbling but quite nice speech, and in the middle of it he looked down at the front row and sort of started and rubbed his eyes and lost the thread of his remarks but recovered it in time and finished his speech, and there were more cheers and the curtain kept going up and down until at last it stayed down and the applause died reluctantly away and people began fishing for their hats and coats.

And then, just as Roger was wondering how to find the stage door and go behind the scenes and look for his father and mother, everything sort of faded and merged and went up like fireworks, and the world turned black. And the next moment he and Ann and Jack and Eliza were sitting in the familiar time garden breathing the scent of the familiar thyme.

"Darn!" said Eliza. "I wanted to congratulate your father!"

"So did I," said Ann, in a small voice.

"So did I," said Roger. "But I guess," he added reflectively, "that would be eating our cake and having it, too."

"We never seem to be able to do that, somehow," said Ann. "Even with magic."

There was a pensive pause.

"I suppose that's the last adventure?" said Jack.

"H'absolutely the h'end!" said the Natterjack.

"Well," said Ann, "it's been just lovely."

"All things considered," said Eliza.

"Thanks a lot," said Jack.

"Good-bye," said Roger, feeling that this sounded inadequate and wondering if he should offer to shake the Natterjack's hand.

"Will we see you again?" asked the tenderhearted Ann, who hated all partings.

"H'I may nod in passing," considered the Natterjack. "But don't h'expect to waste my time in vain conversation and h'idle regrets. I've h'other things to do. Besides," it added, "you won't *be* 'ere very much longer."

"That's so," said Eliza. "Vacation ends next month. I start Latin this year. They say it's awful. You decline nouns. All I can say is, who wouldn't?"

"That," said the Natterjack, "is not precisely what I 'ad in mind." And it hopped away before they could ask it anything more.

It was not until the next day that the four children learned what the Natterjack *did* have in mind, precisely. After breakfast (of a wonderful corn porridge called samp which was one of Mrs. Annable's specialties) old Mrs. Whiton told them that she had had a long cablegram from their parents and that the play was a success.

"Good," said Ann and Roger.

"I thought somehow it might be," said Eliza. And she made a sitting motion to the others, which the others loftily ignored.

And then old Mrs. Whiton went on to tell them a lot more news that had been in the cablegram. It seemed that the London theater people wanted Roger and Ann's father to stay on in England and write another play, a musical play this time, and so Ann and Roger were to go to school in London for a year. And they had talked it over with Uncle John and Aunt Katharine, and Jack and Eliza were to come, too. Jack would go to a boys' school with Roger, and Eliza to a girls' school with Ann.

"Coo Lummy!" cried Eliza, in what she believed

to be British tones. "Now we'll *really* see London! That other was just practice."

"Still it may come in handy," said Ann. "I feel at home there already."

"Ahem," said Roger, with a meaningful glance in the direction of old Mrs. Whiton.

But old Mrs. Whiton, unlike many a grown-up, did not embarrass them by asking what they were talking about, but tactfully changed the subject to that of packing and getting ready to leave in time to catch the boat from New York the following Monday.

And from then on that is mainly what they did. It is amazing how many new possessions may be accumulated by four children in the course of one summer vacation, but a few were eliminated and the rest pushed in on top of other things, and the trunks finally closed.

At last the day of departure came. Old Henry was to drive the children into the village to catch the Boston train. Old Mrs. Whiton said she hated scenes of farewell at railroad stations and would have none of them. Besides, the four children wanted it that way. It seemed right, somehow, to go as they had come. They would change trains in Boston without adult aid, as they had done before, and in New York their Uncle Mark would meet them and take them to his house for the night, before putting them on their ship in the morning. He would arrange official things like passports, too.

On the last morning Mrs. Annable cooked a particularly lavish breakfast and then bade them a terse good-bye. Old Mrs. Whiton added a gruff but affectionate one and followed them out of the house.

"Just a minute," said Ann, suddenly. She ran into the garden and through the opening in the hedge onto the thymey bank. Jack and Roger and Eliza followed. The four stood looking at the leafy green hummocks, and breathing their scent for the last time.

"This is one place we'll never forget," said Roger.

"Will we find any magic in England, I wonder?" said Eliza. "Or is it good-bye to childish folly?"

"A boys' school!" said Jack. "How'll I get to know any English girls?"

The Willys-Knight honked in the driveway. But Ann thought she had seen something moving among the tiny dark green leaves.

"I'll catch up with you," she said, lingering behind as the others turned reluctantly to answer the summons of the horn.

She waited till they were out of earshot. Then she spoke. "Good-bye," she said. "It really *is* good-bye this time. It's been wonderful. Even if we never have any magic again, it was worth it."

Something moved once more among the dark green leaves. Something hopped nearer. The Natterjack looked at Ann. It nodded. Then it passed by, hopping away out of Ann's sight forever.

Ann sighed. There didn't seem to be anything more to say. She ran to catch up with the others.

The last car door slammed. The Willys-Knight roared, shifted gears and purred. The last good-bye died on the breeze.

Old Mrs. Whiton stopped waving. She stood on the steps of the old house, looking up at the sky, where clouds were piling in the northeast. That meant a storm was coming, and old Mrs. Whiton's eyes flashed. She liked storms. They were a challenge to her. She went into the house, and soon her typewriter keys were clacking wildly, furiously, as though the storm were already there and she were racing the wind of it.

But in the garden the sun still shone. The innumerable bees hummed. The scent of thyme hung on the air. But only the Natterjack was there to breathe the fragrant essence of it.

He and the garden were waiting. They were waiting for more children. They didn't care how long they waited. They had all the time in the world.

Edward Eager (1911–1964) worked primarily as a playwright and lyricist. It wasn't until 1951, while searching for books to read to his young son, Fritz, that he began writing children's stories. In each of his books he carefully acknowledges his indebtedness to E. Nesbit, whom he considered the best children's writer of all time — "so that any child who likes my books and doesn't know hers may be led back to the master of us all."